THE LIBRARY

FROM Anna Dabai OF

Anna
Anna Khlébnikova 1770-1843

E. M. ALMEDINGEN

Anna

Illustrated by Robert Micklewright

London
OXFORD UNIVERSITY PRESS
1972

Oxford University Press, Ely House, London W.1

GLASGOW   NEW YORK   TORONTO   MELBOURNE   WELLINGTON
CAPE TOWN   IBADAN   NAIROBI   DAR ES SALAAM   LUSAKA   ADDIS ABABA
DELHI   BOMBAY   CALCUTTA   MADRAS   KARACHI   LAHORE   DACCA
KUALA LUMPUR   SINGAPORE   HONG KONG   TOKYO

First published 1972

ISBN 0 19 271337

PRINTED IN GREAT BRITAIN BY
MORRISON AND GIBB LTD, LONDON AND EDINBURGH

To
John S. G. Simmons, M.A.
of
All Souls College, Oxford,
with deep gratitude
from
Anna's great-grand-daughter
E. M. Almedingen

Contents

Prologue

It was a very hot morning in June, and the scent of freshly cut hay came through the wide-open window on the first floor of a large white stone house. The window gave out onto a round courtyard, with a wide oak avenue beyond. The avenue sloped towards a large meadow. The measured swish-swish of numberless scythes could not reach the house, but the width of the avenue afforded a generous landscape shimmering with colour. The grass suggested swathes of sheer emerald, the curved scythes gleamed silver, the scarlet shirts of the peasants, sleeves tucked well above the bronzed arms, here and there pale blue clumps of cornflowers, and beyond the silver-blue washes of the river . . . It was too hot for the peasants to sing; but the scarlet rows moved in music, rhythm in foot, arm and in measured, accustomed swing of the scythe. A bell rang somewhere; the scarlet phalanx stopped, scythes on the grass, and rough tanned hands busily wiped sweat off faces and necks.

From the open window a little lady in a trim white cap and a grey lawn gown, took off her spectacles, closed her walnut desk and glanced towards the meadow. Every corner of that world was dear and familiar. So was that other world where the little lady had spent the entire morning, a world etched so clearly in her memory when she did not have to wear spectacles, long skirts, and never got tired either of work or play, when she was a bare-footed little girl, two flaxen plaits dangling on her back, the inky left hand rubbing her freckled forehead and the right hand snatching at a cucumber, a shy little girl who had never been inside a country house.

Now the little lady was back in her room at Avchourino. She raised the lid of her writing-desk and leafed over sheets of thick grey paper covered with spidery handwriting.

'Well,' she thought, 'I have done my stint for the day, and I think I would like some well-chilled raspberry water.'

But she did not stretch her tiny hand towards a handbell. She leant back on the chair, which was covered with green damask, and closed her eyes. In a few moments she was fast asleep, the summer wind caressing her face with the fragrance of new-mown hay. Asleep, she was a little girl again, so cherished but never spoilt in her father's house in Moscow.

Well, I have seen that old walnut desk and some of those sheets of thick grey paper. From a wall of my study in England I can see my great-grandmother's face framed in an elegant little cap. She is shown wearing spectacles. The grey-blue eyes seem grave but not forbidding, and the mouth is soft. It is a scholar's face; she was a scholar but she never thought of herself as one.

I have thus imagined her shaping her early memories and putting them down on paper. The manuscript was never meant for publication and has since perished together with many other treasures of Avchourino. But the book is not wholly fiction; its background is based on reality. That little girl spent a happy and busy childhood in her father's house in Kolomna, a suburb of Moscow, shared tutors with her gifted brother, mastered Latin, German and many other languages, delighted in weaving garlands of cornflowers and in the rare picnics to the Sparrow Hills south of Moscow, was devoted to her father and loved all his servants, met the Empress Catherine the Great, and later my very handsome and elegant great-grandfather. But something of the little girl with a passion for learning, horses and apples never died in her. Those are facts.

And I feel I should like to tell her story as I think she would have liked to see it. She was well over sixty when she began 'to scribble'.

E. M. Almedingen

January 15th, 1971.

On the Sparrow Hills

I think I was about five or six when I woke up one sunny May morning to see Fekla, one of the house girls, red-cheeked and buoyant, carrying a jug of ice-cold water from the well.

'Get up, get up,' she cried in her sing-song voice. 'We are off to the Sparrow Hills this morning and the weather is enough to make a donkey sing.'

I was very fond of Fekla. To please her I jumped off my narrow bed, all naked as I was, splashed my face and body with the cold water, slipped into a cotton shift, thrust my feet into linen sandals, pulled a yellow cotton frock over my head, and submitted to Fekla's rather clumsy ministrations with comb and brush. My hair plaited, I asked:

'Is Yasha ready?'

'Indeed he is. He had his bacon and all like a true Christian, your brother did. Here, stand still a minute. There is a grand blue ribbon to go round your head. And the master has ordered the cart and two men.'

'Which?'

'Semka and Ivan,' mumbled Fekla, twisting the ribbon round and round my forehead.

'I like them! Fekla, where is my breakfast?'

She laughed, her pearl-white teeth gleaming.

I stamped my little foot.

'Well?'

'Now, Anna, I have brought you a mug of milk and some wheaten bread. Don't gobble—but eat quickly. The master has gone out and no horse likes to be kept waiting.'

'No,' I agreed solemnly, drank the milk, nibbled at the bread and rushed out of the door to see Yasha, bare-headed, bare-legged, in a grey cotton shirt and white linen breeches.

'Oh Yasha!' I breathed, almost too happy to be articulate. 'Sparrow Hills! And where is Father?'

'Gone to the corn market. Come on, Anna. Agasha is in the
cart. It is going to be a scorching day.'

The clumsy cart was at the door. Semka and Ivan, both
bearded, broad-shouldered and sturdy, smiled at me. I saw
Agasha, my nurse, seated at the back of the vehicle, hampers and
baskets on her right hand and on her left. I was lifted up into the
cart and I could smell the sweet straw under my feet. Then I
heard Semka's voice as he urged the chestnuts. My right hand
clutched in Agasha's plump warm fingers, I leant back and closed
my eyes. I knew and loved my Moscow, but I was on my way to
a glorious day in a shady glade of the Sparrow Hills, and I wanted
to see nothing else.

It was a long drive and I fell asleep. I woke when I felt Semka's
sturdy arms lift me out of the cart. I stared at the glory of beech,
oak and elm all around me. I could not see Yasha anywhere. A
few yards beyond, in a glade shaded by beeches, Agasha and
Fekla were spreading a snow-white cloth on the green grass, and
I saw Ivan carrying up the hampers. From afar off I heard the
faint silver tinkle of running water. The stream? The famous
Sparrow stream. I struggled out of Semka's arms and ran. At the
end of the glade I caught sight of Yasha's grey shirt. I stopped,
breathed greedily and caught up with him. He turned and flung
an arm round my neck. I felt in paradise.

'Yasha! Yasha!' I muttered. 'We'll have games in the wood,
won't we?'

'Of course, Anna. But everything is ready. We had better get
down to dinner.'

'Dinner? I don't want to eat.'

'But you would not like to displease Agasha? Anna, she took
such trouble over the hampers!'

'Oh well,' I pouted, but I followed my brother down the glade.

Agasha, Fekla and the men had spread the snow-white cloth
under the beeches. Just below, the ground ran down to a meadow.
From where we sat, we could see Moscow, all her numberless
belfries glittering in the May sunshine. The white walls of the
Kremlin looked like silver, and the red walls of the China Town
gleamed fiery crimson. Yasha, his bronzed legs sprawled on
the silken grass, pointed out one landmark after another. Seven
years older than I, Yasha, so I thought, knew everything, but
that morning was so heavenly that topography pleased me as

much as a sour apple. I seized Yasha's hand and pulled myself up.

'All right,' he said, 'I'll take you up a hill where the firs are and a tiny waterfall. There should be plenty of wild flowers.'

The uphill path was steep for my little legs. Yasha mended his pace to mine, but I panted and stumbled, and even missed my foothold once. He helped me up but he did not say he was sorry, and even at that early age I liked him for it.

At last the path ended close to the edge of a little glade girdled with rather stumpy firs. To the left, the ground rose sharply, and there was the stream, the water dancing from one stone to another, both banks carpeted with tiny flowers, violet, pink, white, yellow. I did not know their names, I did not want to know them. They were just the kind of flowers for a dolls' garden. Hot, dishevelled and all, I started making one small posy after another—for Agasha, Fekla and two other women, till Yasha stopped me.

'You will never carry them all down. Have a drink now, Anna. That will cool you.'

'But we have no mug with us.'

'Cup your hands, little sister, or else lap it up. Watch me.'

I cupped my palms but icy cold water kept trickling through. So I lay down flat and drank with my mouth. Our chins rubbed dry, we flung ourselves on the grass.

'That water was like the snow we have in winter,' I sighed contentedly—and turned to stare at the glade.

'Oh Yasha, dear, dear Yasha,' I gasped. 'Let us build a hut here and live there all together, have a few fowls and a cock and—'

He shook his head.

'You would not like to spend a single winter here, Anna. Bears prowl about in search of food. Why, Semka said his uncle had seen two wolves near here.'

'Two wolves?' I stared. 'What did Semka's uncle do?'

'Well, I think one of the beasts did not see him. Semka's uncle killed the other with a hatchet.'

'Oh no! I do hate killing.'

'But the wolf would have killed Semka's uncle and eaten him.'

I shuddered. The glade did not look at all attractive.

'And if it had been a bear?'

'Bears are different. They hug you but they don't eat you. It is peas, carrots, berries, apples and honey they like. They have such a sweet tooth, you would not believe it. If you meet a bear among raspberry bushes, he would take no notice of you so long as you left him alone.'

'Have you seen one?'

'More than one, little sister.'

'I shuddered again. Yasha patted my shoulder.

'Don't get frightened. I would never have brought you here if I thought we might meet one. Bears don't like the Sparrow Hills, see?'

'Why?'

'Too many people come here. Any Sunday or feast day you would see a crowd enjoying themselves. And on ordinary days gentry come with their servants and have their victuals in the open air, but not in the mornings, I heard Semka say.'

'Who are gentry?'

'Oh, those grand folk—' Yasha whistled. 'They live in stone mansions and eat off silver plates. I believe their women would not know how to put on their own hose.'

I listened, my mouth wide open. Yasha added, staring at the waterfall:

'They wear silk and velvet. Oh, little sister, they are so rich and they never work.'

'Don't they hem their shifts?'

He laughed.

'Hem their shifts! Anna, they would not know a thing about it. Sometimes,' Yasha lowered his voice, 'I wish we could live in a country where everybody works—just like Father does.'

'But is there such a land anywhere?'

'There will be—some day,' he muttered and seized my hand. 'Little sister, it is time we went down, else Agasha might think we are lost.'

'Yes.' I jumped up and then stooped, remembering to gather up my posies. 'Oh dear, Yasha, I do feel hungry.'

'So do I.'

We got down and found Agasha and Fekla in what I called a taking. Agasha kept stamping her bare foot on the grass. Yasha, she said, had no business to take me so far.

'And just you look at Anna! Plaits all dishevelled and there is a scratch on her knee! Oh dear!'

'We drank such lovely cold water, Nannie,' I said, 'and I have

made posies for you and Fekla and oh, dear goodness, we feel
famished.'

'So you should be,' grumbled Agasha, and smiled, and I knew
everything was all right. Bears, wolves, gentry all slipped out of
my mind. Very greedily I stared at the ground. There, on a clean
homespun white cloth, lay a huge flat pastry, already sliced, and I
could see it had chopped meat and onions inside. There were
some hard-boiled eggs, chunks of rye bread, a big jam tart, a jug
of milk and another of *kvas*. There was no cutlery. We ate with
our fingers, wiping them on the edge of the cloth. We were all
together, Agasha, Fekla, Semka, Ivan, Yasha and I. My mouth
full of the succulent pastry, I heard my brother ask one of the
men:

'You have fed and watered the horses, haven't you?'

Ivan grinned from ear to ear.

'And would we be enjoying our victuals, young master, if I had not. Ah yes, a nosebag for each and two bucketfuls of water. Let them have their fill, God bless them!'

The jam tart finished, we all made the traditional sign of the cross, and Agasha spoke lazily.

'Once we have cleared away, we'll have a nap and then sing a song or two.' Her brown eyes twinkled. 'There is a piece of honey bread in the cart—whoever sings best will get it.'

'That will be Semka,' I sighed.

The cloth was folded. The empty jugs and mugs were carried away to the cart. We six, slightly mazed with fresh air and most blissfully replete, were about to lie down under the shadow of the beeches when the jingle of harness broke upon us. Semka and Ivan stirred. Agasha pulled at her kerchief. Fekla gaped. Yasha raised his head and I saw his mouth curve in a smile. I sat up and stared.

I saw a magnificent coach, painted black and crimson, drawn by four superb chestnuts, their silver harness gleaming. The coachman and the young man beside him wore green and silver livery, their tricornes showing their powdered hair. In the rear rode four postilions, wearing the same livery. The horses reined in. The postilions dismounted. A lacquered door of the coach was flung open. One by one, two girls, slightly older than I, stepped out. They had yellow straw hats over their ringleted hair, pink silk dresses embroidered from throat to hem, white gloves reaching up to the elbow, and high-heeled silk boots. They stepped on the grass and giggled. Behind them came a portly female in a flounced lilac gown and a white bonnet, her hands gloved in pink. Her painted plump face turned towards us, and we heard her broken Russian as she spoke to one of the postilions:

'I thought we were coming too early. Michael, leave the hampers inside. Irina, Elizabeth, kindly get back into the coach. We are going home.'

The magnificent postilion bent his powdered head, but the little girls did not move and they kept staring at us.

'Why should we go?' lisped one of them. 'It is so interesting. Just look—that girl has no hose on her legs! Do they belong to the poor? Mama sends food to them on Sundays! Why, Irina and I have some silver in our pouches—'

'Get back into the coach, Elizabeth,' said the portly female. 'What would the Countess say if I allowed you to have a picnic here? I did think we were coming too early. I suppose these people are artisans or shopkeepers. Elizabeth, Irina, get back into the coach!'

Those incredibly elegant girls pouted but they climbed back into the carriage. The plump female, her lilac skirts rustling, threw a contemptuous glance at us, and mounted the coach. The harness jingled, the horses moved, and all was still again. Agasha closed her eyes and muttered, 'Good riddance to the likes of you.' Fekla began to snore. I tugged at Yasha's shoulder.

'They looked nasty, Yasha. Who were they?'

'Some of those gentry from Moscow, I think,' he muttered.

He spoke as though he did not want to go on, but I clenched my little fists and would not stop.

'They were rude, Yasha! They stared as if we had no business to be here, and those silly girls pointed at the cart and giggled! What is the matter with our cart? Father would not ape such folk by sending us off in a coach.'

'He has no coach.'

'I hate people like them,' I burst out.

'Silly to hate anyone, little sister. The world is made that way. There is the top and there is the bottom.'

'You and Father and I are not the bottom.'

'Of course not—nor yet the top,' Yasha said sleepily, and he closed his eyes.

But, alone among them, I kept awake for a bit. Angry, hurt and bewildered, I wished never to see the Sparrow Hills again. I did not know it at the time, but I had had my first lesson in social divisions. The lesson, however, proved far beyond my little understanding. I wished I had torn those silken gowns to shreds, and I fell asleep, a hot cheek pressed against the grass.

When I woke, I saw Semka and Ivan harnessing the horses. Sitting up and rubbing my eyes, I caught sight of Agasha, a mug in her hands.

'Here is a cool drink for you.'

I drank the beautifully chilled raspberry water and then snatched at Agasha's roughened hand.

'Why, you look all out of sorts, little one.'

'I hate all gentry.'

A.—2

Agasha laughed.

'You are a silly. Why should you?'

'They stared so. They giggled. They looked at us as though we were all worn-out boot soles.'

'Silly again, Anna,' Agasha said in her practical voice, 'and all of us bare-footed too! Come on, child. Time to ride home. And don't you tell the master how foolish you were. Ivan heard what you said to Yasha. Getting into such a tantrum all because of two stupid little girls!'

'Nannie, why should there be a top and a bottom?'

'Well, I guess we folks are like streams and hills, Anna. God knows best, I reckon. But I heard them talk once about a pieman and he ended a prince.'

'And he rode in a coach?'

'I daresay he had a dozen coaches.' Agasha added piously, 'It is all God's will and high fortune. Now, off with you to the cart.'

2

My Paradise

I always called it that—in Russian—*moy ray*, but few people would have called it beautiful. The long, timbered two-storied house, with a humped loft above, gave out straight on the Kolomna road, and was known as 'Khlébnikovs'. Three generations had traded there in seed and corn. The back wall of the house faced a huge yard, with a stone-stepped well in the middle. To the left were stables, store-sheds and oddly shaped buildings for my father's carts. To the left stretched a long, low, timbered building housing his foreman, drivers, workmen, and two shy, weedy clerks, their chins and fingers usually splotched with ink. Beyond the yard, a creaking gate led to the kitchen-garden where cabbages, turnips and onions crowded in amongst a cluster of pear and apple trees. Beyond again stood the *pustósh*, or wilderness, a stretch of land overgrown with scutch and nettles. Its boundary marked the

9

end of Khlébnikovs proper. There was not much of a view, but
many trees grew there, and a profusion of flowers rioted in the
kitchen-garden. How I loved it all.

In front, a stoutly timbered door led to the *seny*, a covered
porch. To the right was a plainly furnished room where the clerks
worked standing at their desks and where my father saw his
foreman, received customers, and signed his papers. To the left
was his sanctum, a big square room crammed with books inherited and bought in Russian, Old Slavonic, German, French,
English, Dutch, Greek and Latin. The room had a table and a few
straight-backed chairs. At the back a narrow door led to another
room furnished with a similar simplicity, where Yasha worked
with his tutors and where later I was allowed to join him.
Somewhere on the right of the narrow unfurnished hall was a door
into the *górnitza*, a long, bare room where we met twice a day to
eat, to pray and sometimes to talk. The kitchen quarters lay
just beyond.

From the narrow hall, perilously steep uncarpeted stairs led to a
landing and a passage opening out to a few rooms—my father's,
Yasha's, mine, and a few guest rooms. An icon in the east corner,
a ewer and a basin standing on a rough unpainted table, a coffer
for clothes, a wooden bed with a flat, hard mattress and as hard a
pillow, and two homespun blankets summed up the furnishing
of my room and Yasha's. Carpets, cushions, sheets and pillow-
cases were unknown. A wealthy merchant's children, we were
brought up hard.

Winter and summer alike, when a clock struck five, Fekla came
in with a tallow candle and a jug of ice-cold water. Washed and
dressed, I would turn to the east corner, make a prostration, cross
myself, and say 'Our Father' and a prayer to the Holy Ghost.
Then I would follow Fekla's candle down the steep stairs. The
rose-red brick stove made the *górnitza* gratefully warm. The bare
oaken table was laid with two jugs of steaming hot milk, a wooden
bowl of red-cheeked apples, three earthenware platters, a dish of
hot flour-powdered *kaláchi*, butter, honey, and a great silver
zhban of home-brewed ale for my father. Yasha would be there
and in a moment we would hear the familiar heavy tread on the
creaking stairs. We would kneel for my father's blessing, kiss his
hand, and sit down to breakfast.

My father was a tall man, not too broad in the shoulders. He always wore the traditional merchant's clothes: a dark blue gown down to the ankles, caught up in the middle by a leather girdle, and square-toed black boots. His unpowdered hair was cut short and swept off his forehead. His beard was brown, long and silken.

The seed and corn business, inherited from his father, was wholesale. The green-painted carts would be laden with sacks each tied neatly with a hempen cord, a round leaden seal carrying the words known all over Moscow and far beyond: 'Piotr Khlébnikov, *Kolómensky Koopetz*', i.e. 'merchant of Koloma'. When at leisure, Yasha and I felt proud to watch the loading. Kolomna was one of the southern suburbs of Moscow, lying on the east bank of the Yanza, a large place boasting an ancient palace, innumerable churches, monasteries, nunneries and merchants' storehouses. There were patches of greenery, mostly elm, fir and birch, a market where you could buy anything from a sucking-pig to a pair of woven hose, and some oddities like a bright blue-roofed long building known as 'Pavlínovye', i.e. Peacocks' Court, standing in its own grounds and girdled by such a thick high paling that we never saw the wonderful birds. I believe their owner lived in St. Petersburg.

In my childhood, Moscow had *pristavy*, i.e. police, hospitals, a state boarding-school for girls and a few private teaching establishments, none of them open to merchants' children. Well away from Kolomna were the Kremlin, its walls snow-white, the China Town, the great markets, and wide streets of stone-built mansions, but there we went seldom. Except for the annual excursion to the Sparrow Hills, our world ended with the west bank of the Yanza and the entrancing German Quarter, known as *Nemétzkaya Slobodá*, inhabited by foreigners, among whom my father had many friends.

I was far too small at the time to understand the reason of our not going further afield. The fact was that Moscow teemed with vagrants, robbers, murderers and 'red cock men', who often set houses on fire, and most dwellings in Moscow were timbered. Later I learned that robbery, murder and arson carried the death penalty. Law was ruthless because criminals were ruthless. My father would not allow us to go as far as the Kolomna market unless we were accompanied by two of his men, armed with heavy pistols and lead-tipped truncheons. At night, our place was always guarded by two men and three enormous shaggy dogs were unchained.

I had never known anyone like my father. He was an excellent businessman, but literature and languages came first with him. Himself self-taught, he engaged teachers for Yasha, most of whom came from the German Quarter. As I got older, I was allowed to join in some of the lessons. Mathematics and the globe reduced me to tears, but languages were so many opened windows in my little life. There should have been six of us but three sisters, born after Yasha, died in infancy, and I cannot even remember their names. Then I came, and a year later I had a tiny brother, christened Pável. He lived about a month and my mother did not survive him for long. My father did not marry again.

He had never been away from Moscow, but he was a most accomplished man. He employed agents to get him books from abroad. He spoke and wrote Latin, Greek, Dutch, German, French and Swedish, and he meant my brother to become a scholar. His piety was very simple. He kept all the ordained fasts, went to Mass and Vespers every week-end and sometimes oftener, but his many friendships with the people in the German Quarter made some people say that he was not wholly Orthodox. I think it was untrue.

Agasha and Fekla looked after us. There was the fat Vlássovna in the kitchen and two or three other women. They all slept in the loft.

We met my father at breakfast. We dined at noon, often by ourselves. We supped early—just the two of us. Then came brightly rayed days when my father, who seldom took supper, would come in, read aloud to us and question Yasha about his lessons. Then we climbed up the stairs, too happy to talk.

I think I was about seven or eight. It must have been a feast day. We had been to a late Mass at the neighbouring church and were about to sit down to a midday meal when my father came in, a sheet of thick grey paper in his hands.

How well I remember that day! It was early autumn and the Kolomna trees were changing colour, but no leaves had yet fallen. The Mass had been a long one. The house, as usual, was fragrant with wax, verbena, lavender, and all the doors, floors and ceilings gleamed under the sun. My father put the letter down by his trencher, crossed himself, smiled at us, and bent to carve the roast goose.

When the meal was finished, he leant back in his chair.

'I have had a letter this morning. Your Aunt Xenia is coming here.'

I said nothing. Yasha muttered:

'Why?'

'She wants to see you both. Now mind your manners, boy.'

'Yes, Father.'

His blessing given, we two fled into the kitchen-garden. Panting, I sank down under an old apple-tree.

'Yasha, Yasha, who is she?'

My brother chewed a blade of bent grass. His voice rang gloomy.

'Our mother's sister. You have never met her. She lives at Tula.'

'Where is Tula?'

'Oh—far away, south of Moscow. Now, little sister, we'll run twice up and down the wilderness and then you must go and get down to your exercise. Monsier Allion said yesterday that you made a mess of *être*. You wrote "*je fussias*" for "*j'étais*".'

'Because "*je fus*" is right,' I said angrily. 'Oh, drat the exercise. It is a holiday, anyhow.'

'Anna!'

Yasha never raised his voice nor stamped his foot, but the grave way he spoke made me mumble:

'All right—all right,' and I followed him twice up and down the wilderness, and then made for our little sanctum, a square, uncarpeted room, its four shelves carrying our study books. There was a table with an iron standish, a bunch of quills, a stack of thick grey paper, and some blue-bound exercise-books. There was a narrow bench for us and a straight-backed oak chair for the master. The single uncurtained window gave us a glimpse of the yard. There was nothing beautiful in that room, and yet how passionately did I love it because I meant to master the languages my father knew and Yasha was learning. From the foreign quarter across the Yanza came Monsieur Allion, elderly and plump, his silver wig always awry and his blue waistcoat lavishly sprinkled with snuff, and he taught us French. Herr Brandt, a teacher at one of the boys' academies, instructed us in German and Latin. A pale cadaverous gentleman by the name of Kroen-

berg gave us the rudiments of Swedish, and a learned monk
appeared two or three times a week to teach Yasha Greek. At
some of the lessons I was not present. I believe there were other
tutors because Yasha had instruction in mathematics and geography. Languages alone gripped me and my father was wise
enough not to force me to learn things I could never understand.

I could not concentrate that day and the French exercise did not
progress very far. The quill laid down, I propped my chin with
both hands and stared out of the window.

Khlébnikovs seldom had visitors to stay. My father's friends,
and he had many, Muscovite merchants and men from the German
Quarter, came to see him of an evening to sup, talk and puff at
their pipes. They forgathered in his book-room. Neither Yasha
nor I was ever invited to join them. We had friends of our own
age, children of my father's men and others, with whom we
played games in the wilderness and whom we entertained with
chilled milk, chunks of gingerbread or *vatrúshki*, sour-cream tarts
made in the kitchen.

Aunt Xenia from Tula! I had an idea that we had crowds of
relations on my mother's side, but they always kept aloof. Most
of them lived far from Moscow. Travelling was not very easy in
those days. There were post horses and inns, but the latter were
neither comfortable nor safe either. I knew that many an innkeeper ended his days on the block or the gallows for having
been hand-in-glove with highwaymen—a curse in my country
then as they are today.

Yasha had said that Tula was far away. My geography being
rather hazy, I got a book off a shelf. Tula was famous for its
forges, *samovár* makers and smiths. Aunt Xenia would not come
here for just a week! Heavens! Was she coming for good? I
scrambled off the bench and went in search of Agasha.

But Agasha and the other women were busy. Father had gone
out and taken Yasha with him. I felt I could not very well run
into the yard and ask the men about my own aunt. There seemed
nothing for it but to get back to the French verbs.

Khlébnikovs was very quiet that day. It being a holiday, the
men were resting, their tasks done. I went on struggling with a
verb when I heard the door creak.

'Queen of heaven,' gasped Agasha, 'still at your books, Anna!'

I felt so cross I did not answer.

'And your eyes are swollen, too! Has anyone been unkind to you?'

'No.'

'Then what is the matter?'

I pushed the standish so roughly that I almost upset it.

'I did want to talk to you and you were busy,' I said sullenly.

'Feast day or no feast day, I have things to do. What is it?'

'Agasha, do you know Aunt Xenia?'

'She came to the master's wedding.' Agasha rubbed her chin. 'With her husband, I mind well. Talk of fattening a goose for Christmas! Ah, dear soul, I reckon the heavenly gates were widened to let him in! May he rest with the saints.' She crossed herself. 'Gave us all a silver coin, he did, and a huge silver *samovár* to the master. Why, the pearls which will be yours some day, Anna, came from your Uncle Efim.'

But I was not interested either in the pearls or in my late uncle.

'For how long is my aunt coming?'

'I could not tell you, child. Tula is not behind your elbow. But don't you go badgering the master.'

'He doesn't like her?'

Agasha shook her forefinger at me.

'Now, Anna, the master is a saint, I reckon. Far too good a man to dislike anyone, and she—your dear mother's own sister. But there you are! There are the master's books and all those friends of his at the German Quarter, and him with all his languages, too . . . Well, and she is that old-fashioned, Anna. Nobody taught her anything, see. And say nothing to Yasha either. He knows nothing about her. I reckon we are unlikely to see much of her in the house. Pilgrimages all day long—plenty of them in the city!'

'Pious? Oh—Agasha, then she must be good.'

My nurse turned towards the door and said over her shoulder: 'Ah, folks say there is a long, long field to cross between piety and goodness.'

She went. Agasha meant much to me, and I did not mention my aunt's visit either to my father or to Yasha. Moreover, it was pleasant to think that, absorbed in her pilgrimages, Aunt Xenia would not spend much time at Khlébnikovs.

About ten days later Yasha and I stood by the opened gates and watched the green carts move towards the Yanza ferry and the Moscow markets. Having waved to the men, we turned back and

Yasha began bolting the gates when we heard the jingle of harness from the southerly direction. We peered through a chink and saw a clumsy red and blue *kolymáza*, drawn by four horses.

'Those beastly gentry,' I muttered.

'It is Aunt Xenia. Let's slip through the back and make for the study.'

I trotted behind him, and said, panting:

'But shouldn't we be in the porch? I mean—'

'Father is at home,' Yasha flung over his shoulder, 'and Mr. Glass is coming soon. We must get ready for him—'

'My English exercise is ready,' I said proudly.

Soon enough we reached our little sanctuary, got out the books we needed, and arranged the standish and quills for Mr. Glass. He was an elderly clerk to some English firm in Moscow, shy, patient and courteous. I preferred him to Monsieur Allion who complained that my knowledge of grammar was *incroyable*, struck the desk with his fist, and sometimes called me *une petite sotte*. Mr. Glass never shouted. He taught mathematics to Yasha and English to us both. My father and he were great friends, and I was very fond of Mr. Glass. That day, I remember, I hoped that the kitchen women would not forget his customary refreshment: a large cup of strong black coffee and two round wheaten rusks known as *baránki*. Mr. Glass's Russian was very poor; he called the rusks '*barany*', which meant 'rams', but we never laughed at him.

Alas, for our precious hour of study that day. There broke a cacophony of thumps in the porch as trunk after trunk were being carried in. We heard my father's deep voice:

'Welcome, Xenia—but we thought you were coming next week, though my women got your room ready.'

There followed a giggle and a shrill voice spluttering:

'Oh, my dear brother, how glad I am to see you at last. Pray, tell the men to be careful with the black trunk—all my icons are in it. Mother Dosiphea said there was a pilgrimage to the Trinity Abbey next week. Please see that my horses and my men are all right. I don't know Kolomna at all. I could order a coach somehow, couldn't I? I'd hate to put you to any trouble, brother. But oh—the roads nearly killed me! I couldn't touch a morsel at those inns, I tell you! Blackbeetles all over the place, and one innkeeper brought me roast pork on a vigil! Infidel, I called him. Praise the saints, I am safe now—'

'What a chatterer,' murmured Yasha in English. I nodded and heard my father's even voice.

'Your black trunk is safely upstairs, sister. It is past the dinner-hour, but what could we offer you?'

'Well, dear brother,' came the shrill voice, 'back in Tula Mother Dosiphea and Father Mitrofan said I was to fast through the journey because of the pilgrimage, but I have done travelling, haven't I? Well, some hot tea and wheaten bread, perhaps, with a piece of cabbage pastry, and a pickled herring or two won't hurt me, and a slice of gammon, perhaps. And I am partial to raspberry jam with my tea! Why, I feel nearly starving, brother. The prices inns charge you! I declare the government should forbid it. A whole silver rouble I had to pay for a piece of tough beef, a cucumber and a slice of apple tart so stale I would not offer it to a beggar. One silver rouble, brother,' the shrill voice wailed on. Then we heard Agasha marshalling the guest up the stairs, and our dear Mr. Glass appeared.

But, the lesson over, Mr. Glass left rather hurriedly, and Agasha, her mouth grim, summoned us to the best parlour even though there was an ink blotch on my chin and Yasha's hands were grubby. We went in and saw a plump rosy-cheeked woman in the traditional merchant-woman's dress: a blue scarf on her head, a grey *sarafán* reaching down to her knees and falling well over a wide grey kirtle. She was busily finishing a piece of apple tart, looked up and smiled.

'Yasha! Anna! my dears! I have brought gingerbread for you and some nicely painted spoons from the Tula fair.'

We came near the table and as custom demanded, we knelt and kissed her hand. She leant forward and planted a rather moist kiss on our foreheads. As we got up, I saw that her eyes were green and narrow, her cheeks plump and her mouth pursed. I did not like her.

'You were not in the porch when I came in,' she said.

'We were helping to close the store-house,' Yasha said glibly. 'The carts had just left for the market.'

I blushed and bent my eyes, but Aunt Xenia seemed pleased, and delivered herself of a homily. It was good and pious to hear of children helping their elders. We listened in silence. Then we thanked her for the gingerbread and painted wooden spoons she had brought, and ran across the yard into the kitchen-garden.

'How long has she come for?' I asked Yasha. 'That *kolymáza* of hers had enough luggage for a year!'

'Her Dosipheas and Mitrofans would know! But don't fret, little sister. I heard Father tell Agasha the visitor will be flying from one pilgrimage to another. Why, he has hired a coach for her. Our carts would not do.'

I laughed.

Days flew and turned into weeks. We hardly saw anything of our aunt. She usually left Khlébnikovs at dawn for the first mass somewhere, broke her fast at a nunnery, paid one visit after another to the numberless shrines of Moscow, dined with Abbess Glafira, whom we did not know, and attended vespers somewhere. Otherwise, Aunt Xenia went on pilgrimages, sometimes as far as Trinity Abbey. On such occasions she changed shoes for heavy boots and carried a stick.

It was obvious that we did not interest her at all. I think she had an idea that Yasha was going to succeed my father in the business, that is, if she ever thought of him at all. I was the only daughter and a suitable bridegroom would be found when the right time came. I once heard her say to Agasha:

'That niece of mine is sure to have a good dowry. I wonder if my brother has a comely lad in view—someone in the mercers' line, I think.'

Agasha bowed and did not answer.

To Yasha and me, Aunt Xenia seemed someone out of a folk-lore story. Rarely enough she broke bread with us, and it was hard for Yasha and myself not to giggle because we knew well the women's talk in the kitchens.

'Now, then,' Agasha or Fekla might say to the head cook, 'the master's sister-in-law is in to dinner today. Mind you bake enough sour-cream pastries and stuff the turkey with walnuts, too. The pork—'

Vlassovna wiped her glossy red cheeks.

'I had better dress the whole pig today,' she guffawed. 'Queen of heaven! Piety and greed! I reckon she costs dear to those holy abbesses of hers! Now then, Dashka,' she called to one of the maids, 'fetch me twenty eggs to bake for the first course.'

In the *górnitza*, Aunt Xenia enjoyed her food and entertained my father.

'I am in heaven here, brother. Why yesterday I visited seven

monasteries at the Kremlin and attended Vespers at the Novo-
díevechy! Ah but the nuns' choir makes you feel you are among
angels! And the Chudov cathedral with the shrine of St.
Hermogen. Truly, brother, holy Moscow is the mother of all our
cities.'

'I was born here, sister,' replied my father and replenished her
platter with more roast pork. Aunt Xenia beamed on him.

'Tomorrow being a vigil, I shall attend all the Hours at Abbess
Glafíra's,' she said conversationally.

'Don't weary yourself out, sister.'

'Ah, but who could get tired of prayer and singing? And I
have heard folk say that the Tsarina—God save her—is as pious
as any Christian though she was not bred here. Where did she
come from, brother?'

'From Anhalt-Zerbst, sister. Tsarina Elizabeth chose her as
bride for her nephew, the late Tsar Peter. The Tsarina is a most
enlightened lady, sister. Have you not heard that she has founded
boarding-schools for noblemen's daughters, one here in Moscow
and another in St. Petersburg. The girls are taught music, foreign
languages and many other things.'

Aunt Xenia stopped discussing her pork.

'But what an odd notion, brother! Why should girls be taught
their letters, I ask you?'

'Our Tsarina thinks it a good notion.'

Aunt Xenia sighed.

'Ah well, she is a foreigner still,' she said rather sadly, and it was
generous of my father not to tell her that his own little daughter
knew her letters in four languages, and shared daily lessons with
his son.

When the meal was over, we two escaped into the wilderness
and laughed until tears trickled down my cheeks.

Yasha and I were not heathens; we went to Mass on Sundays
and great feasts; we fasted whenever a fast was appointed, said
prayers morning and evening, and made our confession and
communion in Holy Week. We loved the Zaútrenia, the Easter
night service with its triumphant 'Christ is risen, alleluia. Verily
is He risen, alleluia.' We loved the green birch procession in the
morning of Trinity Sunday. A monk instructed us and I knew
and loved one or two nuns in the neighbourhood. But Aunt
Xenia's wallowing in a world of shrines, wax candles, endless

pilgrimages and so on left us at once bewildered and amused. We had a shrewd idea that our aunt had no knowledge of my father's friendship with foreigners in the German Quarter. They came to Khlébnikovs seldom enough and during her stay they never appeared at all.

'We are infidels, Yasha, we are infidels,' I chanted, leaping up and down the wilderness. 'You and I are being taught by foreigners and I know Father does not mean you to go into the trade.'

We stretched ourselves out on the rough grass, and I remembered Aunt Xenia telling us about a hermitage near Tula.

'Father Sofronius lives there,' she had told us. 'Such a holy man he is, keeps the vow of silence, never washes, spends hours on his knees, lives on water, crusts and berries, and sleeps in a stone coffin.'

'That hermit of hers,' I now told Yasha, 'must stink to heaven! Fancy never having a wash! Oh, Yasha dear, do you think Aunt Xenia will end as a hermit?'

'Her? Never! Far too fond of stuffed turkey she is.'

All in all, it would have been a most amusing visit if it were not for the end.

I think it happened in early August. Yasha, I remember, had gone to the German Quarter to see a master of ours. My father had left early for the Arbat market. Aunt Xenia was supposed to drive to the Donskoy monastery, but a messenger called to say that the ceremony had to be postponed because of the Abbot's illness. I did not know about it. Monsieur Allion was coming that day, and I slipped into our study to wrestle with an exercise when the door opened.

It was Aunt Xenia.

'What are you doing here, niece,' she almost hissed at me.

I got up from the bench and I saw that she was angry. I put my hands behind my back.

'I am doing my French exercise, Aunt Xenia.'

'Your what?' she spluttered.

'My French exercise. The master is coming here in an hour.'

'You—you stand there and tell me that you have been taught your letters.'

'In four languages, Aunt Xenia.'

She stalked into the room. I felt frightened but I did not move. I could hear her breathing.

'Don't you answer me back, you insolent child.'

'I am being given these lessons because my father wishes it—'

'Did you not hear me? Answering me back! Here is for your impudence.'

The plump hand hit my right cheek and my left. She hit hard and I screamed from pain and then she started pulling at my hair.

'That will teach you, girl! Answering your elders! What are the women about? You should be set to praying, hemming and darning.'

She stopped hitting me. My cheeks flaming, I drew back:

'Go and say it to my father, Aunt Xenia.'

Her eyes narrowed. Her lips pursed unpleasantly. I had thought her rather stupid, boring with her endless pious talk, and incredibly greedy. But I had seen her kind and generous. Now Aunt Xenia looked and behaved like a stranger. Fleetingly I knew myself glad that Yasha was not there. I also knew that my knees were shaking. I was engulfed in fear but in a fury that such a woman should sit in judgement on my beloved father. I heard her shrill voice:

'Say it to your father, chit? So I shall. Bringing you up as though you were an infidel! For you to take lessons from a man and that man a foreigner! Oh Queen of heaven! The shame of it.'

I heard and stepped forward. I was small. My arms were thin and bony, but Yasha had taught me wrestling and hitting in the proper way. I clenched my right fist hard and struck Aunt Xenia across the mouth. I must have hit hard because a few drops of blood trickled down her chin. She was so taken aback that she staggered toward a book-shelf.

'You'll pay for that, girl,' she panted, fumbling for a handkerchief to wipe her chin. 'Striking your own mother's sister. A mortal sin that is, but you'll pay for it with a good whipping. And a hard penance, too! Why, Mother Dosiphea would have kept you a month on dry bread and water—' Still panting, Aunt Xenia stumbled towards the chair behind the master's desk. 'Infidel!' she hissed. 'That is your heathen learning, girl. Oh Lord, have mercy on Holy Russia—'

I stayed where I was and I said nothing. Neither of us heard the door open. Then I heard my father's deep voice:

'What are you doing here, sister?'

'Why, brother, I just looked in and found Anna meddling in books,' Aunt Xenia said quickly. 'I told her she had no business to be here, was I not right? Well, I slapped her and she hit me.' She made great play with her stained handkerchief.

My father's voice was quiet.

'Anna's business was to be in this room and do her exercises. Sister, I don't allow anyone to slap my daughter. Is that clear?' Here his deep blue eyes turned towards me. He did not smile but he spoke kindly:

'Go outside, Anna, and wash your face.'

I slipped out, ran to the well, cupped both hands under the icy cold water, rubbed my cheeks with my kirtle, and left the yard for the blessed solitude of the wilderness. So bewildered and exhausted did I feel that, having tumbled down, I fell asleep. It was Yasha who woke me, tugging at my shoulder.

'Goodness, Anna! We have looked for you everywhere. Get up for mercy's sake and come into the house. Why, we are supping with Father tonight.'

I got up but I looked defiant.

'I am not going in to supper, Yasha. I could not bear it! Brother, she said such dreadful things about Father, she slapped me and pulled at my hair and called us infidels, and—and I hit her back. Her mouth bled, Yasha.'

'No harm done,' said my brother cheerfully. 'And you need not look like a kitten about to be drowned. She is gone, little sister.'

'Gone?'

'Yes. Father ordered a chaise for her, and she has gone post, trunks and all. Thank heaven, too. Agasha told me she had heard him say that he would not have a child of his mishandled. Aunt Xenia wailed and wailed, but Father had his way. She has gone and she will never come back again. Come on, Anna, stop looking like a trapped rabbit. And you might ask Fekla to make you tidy—'

'But, but, Yasha,' I stammered, 'I—I hit Aunt Xenia.'

'She must have asked for it,' replied my brother.

The episode was finished. Aunt Xenia, back at Tula, never sent another message. At Khlébnikovs nobody mentioned it. To

my astonishment I never had a scolding from my father. Out-
wardly, life slipped back into its earlier routine. But, inwardly,
keeping my bewilderment to myself, I knew I was standing at a
crossroads. Kolomna, Moscow, its churches, sanctuaries, hills and
rivers were my world. The German Quarter on the west bank of
the Yanza, inhabited by the French, English, Dutch, Italian,
Scotch and German experts in art, science and handicrafts, that,
too, was part of the world I knew and loved. Sophie Kroenberg,
daughter of one of our masters, was a friend. So were many others.
I felt both proud and grateful that my father should have had me
taught letters and foreign languages.

But Aunt Xenia! As purely bred a Russian as myself! That she
should have called me an infidel hurt me deeply. I could not share
my bewilderment with either Agasha or Fekla and, obviously, my
father had instructed them not to speak of it to me. Somehow I
could not share my tumultuous thoughts with Yasha and even less
so with my father.

Then one mild autumn morning an idea came to me.

At some distance from Khlébnikovs stood an ancient Donskoy
monastery. There we sometimes went to Mass and all the services
in Holy Week. There I made my yearly confession and took my
communion. I knew none of the monks except Father Tikhon
who heard my confession. He was an elderly man, tall and spare.
His grey eyes looked grave but kindly. I knew him to be a scholar.
Twice a week Yasha went to the Donskoy for his Greek lessons.
Father Tikhon kept the rule strictly and never came to Khlébnikovs, and I knew Yasha thought the world of him.

I was a very ignorant little girl. I just knew that people did not
usually go to confession in the autumn. I saw a number of women
worshippers at the Donskoy but, a service ended, they made for
the gates, and I could not remember ever seeing a single monk
along the long drive fringed by tall limes. For all I knew, women
and girls were not allowed anywhere except that lovely dim
church.

Still I made up my mind to speak to Father Tikhon. Neither
Yasha nor I ever got any pocket-money, but there came occasional
presents on Easter Day and for the Kolomna fairs. I rummaged
in my chest, found four large silver coins, and took two of them
to lay out on candles at the Donskoy.

The old church was empty. Its windows were too narrow and

small to admit much daylight, but so much candlelight glimmered here and there that I found no difficulty in finding my favourite icons. I knelt in prayer to Our Lady of Vladimir, St. Dimitry and St. Michael, found the money box, dropped in my coins, and stuck four fat wax candles into the empty sticks. Then I heard steps shuffling towards me.

It was a bent-shouldered old monk whom I did not know. From under the bushy grey eyebrows his eyes stared at me. The stare was not particularly friendly, and my heart all but missed a beat.

'Blessed be the Lord,' he said, and I mumbled hurriedly:

'For ever and ever. Amen.'

A pause followed. Then I gathered up my sadly frayed courage.

'Please, Father, I have come—I have come—' I gulped and plunged in:

'Could I see Father Tikhon? He knows me. I am Anna Khlébnikova.'

'You mean—confession?'

'No, no,' I hurried.

'Women are not allowed in the monastery,' the old man said dryly.

'I know, Father,' I stammered.

'You wait here, and I'll fetch him,' and he shuffled away.

Then I wished I had not come. I loved the old church but it did not seem the right place to talk about Aunt Xenia. 'I had better go,' I thought, knelt once again in front of an icon and turned towards the porch, when a voice I knew checked me.

'Why, you—Anna? Is Yasha ill?'

I stumbled forward. Father Tikhon blessed me and I kissed his hand.

'You are shaking, child. Are you ill?'

'No, no,' I muttered, 'but—but I want to tell you something, Father—'

His bony hand clutched my elbow.

'I can't take you into the monastery—but we have a garden and there are benches there. Come, Anna.'

The Donskoy garden behind the church may have been beautiful, but I did not see any of it. Father Tikhon brought me to a bench and asked gently:

'What is troubling you, child?'

And it all poured out. The last word spoken, I looked up. Father Tikhon sat very straight, his thin hands stroking his long silver beard, his eyes on an old oak to the right of the bench. I waited.

'Now, Anna, first of all, there is right and wrong in every case. See what I mean? Your aunt was wrong to hit you and call you names, and you were wrong to hit back. But your aunt is old-fashioned. She has spent her whole life in the provinces, and her world does not move, child. She came to Moscow for religious duties. She must have been bewildered by some of your father's ways. You see, Anna, there are many people like your Aunt Xenia to whom anything foreign comes from the devil. In her world, little girls like you aren't taught their letters or anything. You did not know that, did you? Now you were wrong, very wrong, to strike her, and you were right to stand up for your father. I know him and respect him. I share many of his views. I am sure that by the time you have grown up, Russian girls will be educated. But remember, Anna, your aunt belongs to the old school. Women like her do much good. She is wealthy. She cares for the old, the sick, the wretches kept in prison. She was right according to the light given her, and so were you. Is that clear?'

'Yes, Father Tikhon.'

He turned towards me.

'And don't go on being miserable, Anna. Get on with your lessons. Enjoy your games. And never forget one thing—'

'What?'

'That the Lord loves you whatever you are or do. And He loves your aunt with all her pilgrimages and her gluttony. Don't forget there are many mansions in heaven. It is for Him to choose His tenants, not for us. Now I think I have a pupil waiting. God bless you child.'

He got up and blessed me. I went back to Khlébnikovs, my bewilderment resolved. That evening I included Aunt Xenia in my prayers.

A Narrow Escape

Trinity Sunday was, and is, a great annual occasion. Laity's Mass was always earlier than usual because a long Te Deum in honour of the Trinity followed it. From Khlébnikovs we attended it at St. Praskovia's, an ancient humpy little church of a nunnery where the old icons were framed in wood and tallow candles could be bought since wax was too dear for the sisters. The church was served by old Father Vassily, whose very pure voice belied his years. He had a slightly younger deacon whose way of intoning the litanies was enough to deafen you. The choir consisted of some twenty nuns who sung thinly but purely. Yasha and I were devoted to St. Praskovia's. Somehow, it seemed a home for all its poverty. The walls bulged alarmingly here and there, some of the narrow windows were not glazed and the so-called Royal gates, leading into the altar, were daubed with dull crimson and pallid blue. The deacon's vestments were shabby, and Father Vassily's chasubles were rather clumsily patched. The congregation who lit the tallow candles in front of their favourite icons, came from the poorest hovels in Kolomna. But there was something in the old church that quietened you as soon as you came in.

Both Father Vassily and his vociferous deacon were widowers, and the law did not permit them to marry again. Neither had any children. The deacon lived in a lean-to adjoining the east end of the church and Father Vassily had a small hut at the back. I am sure both would have starved if it were not for the nuns and my father. No pilgrims ever came to St. Praskovia's. It had neither a shrine nor a miraculous icon, and Father Vassily was no beggar to haunt the thresholds of the well-to-do Kolomna merchants, who preferred to take one of the Yanza ferries and make for one of the more important sanctuaries in Moscow. A little away from Khlébnikovs stood a big timbered house of a wealthy wool-merchant whose wife would be driven to the Kremlin two or

three times a week, and was known to enthuse over the glories
of St. Basil's Cathedral. 'Such icons and shrines, and the singing!
I declare I took no fewer than fifty wax candles with me last time
I went there. That is a church to bring you close to the heavenly
gates.'

Yasha and I did not think so. We had both been to the Kremlin
and felt awed by the beauty of its cathedrals and abbeys and
palaces. But we belonged to Kolomna; we were the children of a
Kolomna merchant and the humbler glories of the Donskoy
monastery satisfied us.

I think I was eleven or twelve that year. Easter came late, and
the birches would be in young leaf in good time. Their branches
marked Trinity Sunday. The humblest hut at Kolomna was
adorned by them. At Khlébnikovs, every room in the house had
a branch in each corner, so that you smelt spring and summer
wherever you went. I was still rather hazy about my theology, but
Trinity Sunday meant first and foremost the brave radiance of
young birch branches. Those timidly uncurling leaves rustled in
the wind and spoke of a victory of summer over the wintry
rigours.

Agasha and Fekla toiled hard for weeks. My father must have a
new dark blue gown for the great day; a Dutch tailor from our
dear German Quarter contrived a new *carsol* for Yasha, a short-
coat of light grey cloth adorned with green facings and silver
buttons. I had a new white dress reaching down to my ankles.
It was made of linen, and Fekla embroidered green leaves on the
collar and sleeves. My plaits were to be tied with green ribbon
and a narrow green sash encircled my waist. 'All in honour of the
Blessed Trinity,' said Agasha, busily plaiting my hair. 'Don't jerk
your head so, Anna.'

I said impishly:

'I suppose my Aunt Xenia has a dozen pilgrimages today.'

Agasha frowned and did not answer.

We walked to St. Praskovia's for the Mass and the Te Deum.
We broke our fast on the bank of the Yanza, and I bit into my
hard-boiled egg with pleasure. I knew what was coming. Barges,
gay with birch branches, ran up and down the river, and my
father had booked seats for us on board one of them. The barges
would moor at the west bank, we were to go and dine with the
Glasses, visit some other friends, sup with the Allions, and come

home in the evening. All in all, a heavenly day! As I finished my
milk, I looked at my father. He smiled and I smiled back.

Breakfast over, we moved to the tiny timbered jetty and saw
the barge, gay with birch branches, ploughing upstream. We
were not alone on the jetty. Quite a few people crowded behind
us and, turning, I saw the wool-merchant's wife, fatter than ever
in a bright green *sarafán* and a white kirtle flowing down to her
ankles, her plump cheeks pink and moist.

'She should be at some Kremlin sanctuary,' I thought, and
whispered to Yasha:

'There is a ferry. Why, she would upset the barge!'

'Nonsense, little sister,' he muttered back.

I was not so certain. The Yanza, though far more narrow than
the Moskva, ran deep enough in places, and even the Moskva
was known to break her banks during the spring floods. We always
went by barge to the west bank of the Yanza. Early enough my
father and Yasha had taught me to keep still when on board one
of those barges. The well-planed strakes were comfortable
enough, but the gunwales were low and Agasha always had me
settled amidships.

The barge came alongside, but the men had to steady her when
the wool-merchant's wife came aboard and planted herself
amidships. Some two or three friends of hers, obviously strangers
to the city, sat just behind her, and she turned right and left, one
fat pink hand pointing out the various landmarks. The Yanza
ran smoothly enough and there was not much wind. The barge
streamed past the meadow leading to the German Quarter. At
that point the Yanza curved sharply to the east where the blue
and grey walls of a nobleman's mansion gleamed bright under the
May sun and some dozen or so thatched huts stood a little away
from a well-laid-out park.

The bright green *sarafán* grew very excited.

'That is Lobchino,' she said proudly. 'Look, look! There are
peacocks and fantails too. And all the windows are curtained in
velvet. My cook's niece is in service there. She says over two
hundred people sometimes sit down to their meat.'

So excited was she that she started gesturing with both hands
and, finally, got up, slipped, clutched at the gunwale and fell
overboard. The barge shook from prow to stern. People took to
screaming. I closed my eyes. The man at the tiller and the men at

the rowlocks struggled all they could, but the barge, her burden lessened and her mood anything but amiable, lurched ahead and swung to and fro until I knew my feet were soaked. I opened my eyes. I could not see the bright green *sarafán*, but I saw Agasha's face whiter than her headscarf. I heard shrill voices urging people to be quiet. I saw two stalwart oarsmen fling off their red smocks and plunge into the water.

'Overturned! The barge is overturned,' I thought and screamed, 'Father, Yasha, Agasha, Fekla, jump out all of you—' and my legs deep in water seeping into the barge, I crawled to the gunwale and jumped. The flat bank had seemed near enough whilst I was on board. Now it suggested the end of the world. From somewhere afar off I heard a shriek: 'Anna, Anna,' and then the waters

of the Yanza reached up to my waist and neck, swept over my face, and everything vanished.

I came round in an unfamiliar room, but I had no interest in the surroundings. My right hand moved, pinched my cheek, and I knew I was not dead. But the white dress, so carefully ironed by Fekla, was not there. Instead, my body was covered by a soft pale-yellow silk shift. I felt my legs. They were dry. So was my hair. I raised myself on an elbow and stared at the room.

Never had I seen anything like it!

It was square; its two windows were framed in folds of sapphire velvet, and the thick carpet was of the same colour. The high walls were panelled in some honey-tinted wood. Gilt-framed pictures hung between them and narrow long mirrors framed in crystal. To the right of the windows were two doors, their wood darker than that of the walls, and each had delicately painted porcelain medallions in the upper parts. There were two or three armchairs, covered in sapphire velvet, their curved arms and legs gilded. I saw an oval table, its top painted with roses and lilies. I found myself lying on a sofa upholstered in sapphire velvet, a silk cushion under my head.

I stared at it all and I sniffed. The room smelt of a scent I could not recognize. Folds of pale grey stuff concealed the view from the windows. I pinched myself again.

'I am not dead. So it can't be paradise—but where am I?' and I remembered the bright green *sarafán*, the madly lurching barge—with my father, Yasha, Agasha and others on board. I swung my legs off the sofa and I yelled. That strange room seemed more frightening than the waters of the Yanza!

I waited. All seemed very still, and I had no courage to cross the room and turn the door-handle. I sat on the edge of that sofa and I yelled again. Presently one of the doors opened and I saw Yasha. I would have run to him but my legs seemed turned to straw. He came across.

'Don't make such a noise, little sister.'

'Yasha.' I clung to him and sobbed, 'Where is Father and where are Agasha and the others?'

'Father got a wetting, but he is all right. Agasha and the others too. That fat woman,' went on Yasha, 'looked done for when they fished her out, but she is all right now.'

'And what about you?'

Yasha grinned.

'I am all right. You looked like a drowned minnow, little sister, but they rubbed you dry and warm.'

'Was—was anyone hurt?' I asked shakily.

'No. The men brought the barge alongside all right. There was no need for you to jump, silly Anna.'

'Yasha, where are we?'

'Why, at Lobchino. The green *sarafán*,' Yasha said mischievously, 'rather hoped to spend the night here, but they mopped her up and sent her back in a coach.'

'Yasha, I had never imagined there were such houses! Velvet and mirrors and all! Look what they have put on me! Silk and lace and flounces everywhere. I feel like a changling.'

'Agasha is here,' my brother broke in. 'All your clothes are clean and dry. Father went back to Khlébnikovs as soon as he knew you were warm and safe. He is sending a cart for us. We'll use the ferry to cross the Yanza. I am sorry for poor Grishna—few people will care to use his barge, but he should never have let that green *sarafán* come on board. Why, she was just like a whale!'

'And our Trinity Sunday supper has gone up the chimney,' I sighed.

'It has not. We'll have it at home. And there will be music, dancing and singing in the yard! Now, little sister, when Agasha has made you tidy, tell her, please, that you want to see the housekeeper and thank her, will you?'

'Yes, Yasha, but is there no one else? I mean—who does the house belong to?'

'Some highly placed gentry. You are so fond of them, aren't you?' Yasha grinned. 'But they don't come here often. They live in St. Petersburg. There will be nobody for you to see except the housekeeper.'

'Don't come here often?' I echoed. 'And it is all so beautiful!'

'Is it?' My brother looked about the room and whistled. 'Well, for my part I prefer Khlébnikovs. I'll wait for you in the grounds, little sister,' and he vanished.

Presently Agasha appeared, her arms laden with my clothing. She flung it all on the nearest chair, crouched by the sofa, stroked my face, wept, hugged me and kissed me.

'Anna, Anna, little one, my treasure! God was merciful.'

I kissed her back and wriggled out of her arms.

'I was nowhere near drowning, Nannie. I was just—well foolishly frightened and the water did not taste nice either.'

'Ah, my little pigeon! Queen of heaven, be praised.'

My hair combed, my clothes put on, I remembered my brother's message.

'Nannie, Yasha said I was to thank the housekeeper for her kindness to me.'

'She is waiting outside,' Agasha replied rather shortly and opened one of the two doors. I saw a wide passage, its floor carpeted in crimson, its walls panelled in white. I saw a slim fair woman, hardly older than Agasha, standing at the end. She wore what we used to call 'German' clothes, a grey gown tight at the

top and billowing down to her ankles. For a kerchief she had a
piece of wispy lace on her brown hair, and her neckline and cuffs
were edged with lace. Yet it was not just her clothes but her
manner and her face that drew me to her. She advanced un-

hurriedly but eagerly, her hands folded at her waist, her shapely
head held up. The oval face with its dark blue eyes and soft
mouth looked truly and warmly Russian for all the 'German'
clothes she wore. 'Why, I could make a friend of *you*,' I thought.

'Anna,' I heard Agasha say, 'this is Mavra Akimovna who was
so kind to you when they brought you in.'

I remembered my manners, bowed from the hips, and said
clearly:

'Thank you for all your kindness, Mavra Akimovna.'

To my bow the woman replied with a curtsy, and I wondered

if she could have been in service somewhere in the German Quarter. Never before had I seen a Muscovite woman curtsy.

The cart was waiting, with Yasha seated by the driver. I believe the doors were flung open by flunkeys in crimson and white, but I took no notice of them. Once in the cart, I muttered to Agasha:

'I liked her, Nannie, but why ever did she wear those clothes?'

'Ah, little one, her master must belong to the foreign set.'

'Agasha, you talk like my Aunt Xenia! And who does the house belong to?'

'How should I know? They carried you there, half drowned, my pet, and they treated you kindly.'

I asked no more questions, and I did not tell my faithful Agasha that for a reason I could not understand the house-keeper's image was engraved in my memory. She had not uttered a word but her very silence was sadly eloquent. It was as though she had said time and time again: 'Welcome home.'

The cart reined in. I was back at Khlébnikovs and all thoughts about Lobchino flew out of my mind. The afternoon was closing in and the evening promised to be fair and mild. The men were stringing up oil lanterns here and there on the walls of the great yard, and wide trestles were carried out of doors. The men's work done, the women, led by Agasha and Fekla, came into their own. The trestles were covered by snow-white cloths, and the women called to the men to bring the benches. From a back-door I watched the trestles set out for the Trinity supper. In among branches of young birch stood the big jugs of beer, raspberry *kvas* and something else. There were large bowls of creamed cucumber soup, huge *pirógi* stuffed with cabbage and mushrooms, hard-boiled eggs, and suchlike-food I was accustomed to since my childhood. We had flat wooden platters, wooden spoons and horn-handled knives.

When all was ready, my father came in, crossed himself twice and sat down in the middle of a bench. All the men and women hurried up. The last crumb eaten, the women removed the cloths and Semka started a song about a Persian princess on an enchanted island. Ivan brought out his balalaika and gave us a tune. Then one of the men, born somewhere in Ukraina, led us all in a chorus of a song I had never heard before. The same man

sang the battle-song of the Cossacks. One line only still lingers in
my memory:

'For the honour of our faith and the beauty of our land—'

As the shadows deepened, the lamps were lit; men, women and
girls ran into the yard for the dancing, and I danced 'Russkáya'
with Yasha. From time to time I glanced towards the trestle
where my father sat, stroking his long beard and sipping raspberry
water out of a tall clear goblet a friend had brought him from
Venice. At the other end of the trestle, Agasha, her pale blue
sarafán gleaming silver in the lamplight, leant her elbows on the
table, a nut between her fingers.

Then, hot and breathless, my plaits in a wondrous disorder, I
made for the trestle and nearly emptied my father's goblet. He
smiled and stroked my head.

'Sit down, little daughter. None the worse for your wetting,
are you?'

'Oh no, Father.'

I nestled close to him and watched the dancing. The men wore
white smocks and blue breeches, their legs were bare, and they
wore bast sandals tied up by home-made leather thongs. The
women and girls were all in traditional *sarafáns*, the best ones put
on in honour of the feast, their strings of *boússý*, multi-coloured
glass beads, jingling and flashing whenever the lamplight caught
them. They did not dance to music; from time to time the men
would stop, raise their hands and clap them for several seconds.

I watched breathlessly. They had never been taught any
dancing. They had it in their blood. I had often watched people
at it during our very occasional visits to the Kolomensky or
Prechistensky fairs. But that Sunday evening, at Khlébnikovs, I
thought that my Aunt Xenia could have joined in the dancing.
She, too, had it in her blood. Were it not for her fear of and
contempt for foreigners and her dreadful temper, I thought that
I might have come to love her. I watched Agasha replenish
my father's goblet. For no reason at all, I remembered the housekeeper at that magnificent mansion.

'Father,' I asked suddenly, 'to whom does that grand place
belong—you know—where they brought me to?'

'Some nobleman or other,' he replied, his eyes on the dancing.
'But the family hardly ever live there. It is always St. Petersburg
and its suburbs for them.'

'Their housekeeper wore "German" clothes,' I went on, 'and there were men-servants in short red velvet coats and white breeches!'

My father laughed.

'Little daughter, everybody wears what you call "German" clothes—except merchants and peasants. Surely you know that. Tzar Peter—God rest him with the Saints—brought that in.'

I nodded.

'I did like that housekeeper. I thanked her. Mavra Akimovna her name is. I hope I may meet her again. So kind she seemed. I expect she would be happy to wear a *sarafán*.'

My father laughed again, and heard me stifle a yawn.

'To your prayers and bed, little daughter,' he said, got up, stooped and traced the sign of the cross on my forehead. I bent low, kissed his hand, and slipped away. I fear my prayers were rather scrambled that night.

4

Yasha Starts Travelling

The busy years slipped by. I was thirteen, and my passion for languages burned higher than ever. My geography and history were a little less sketchy than they used to be. But arithmetic still brought me to the verge of tears. I would bite my underlip and my thumb, try as hard as I could, but not the simplest sum ever came right.

One morning Agasha, herself illiterate, brought me a small piece of thick grey paper.

'Petka, the shoe-maker's boy, has just brought it. There are the master's felt house boots, your red leather shoes, and some sandals for Fekla and Dashka. I have money and to spare in the chest, but what does it come to, Anna? The master is out and so is Yasha.'

I pushed away my Tacitus and stared at the bill. The shoe-maker must have employed a clerk to write it so neatly. The figures looked clear enough. I snatched at a quill and started adding them up. After the fourth attempt, my eyes swimming in tears, I looked up at Agasha.

'It is no good, Nannie. Father's shoes cost one rouble eighty copecks, and mine—two roubles, and the sandals come to ninety copecks. I do know there is one hundred copecks to a rouble, but every time I add it up, it comes out differently. I am such a fool!'

Agasha picked up the paper.

'Don't you start fretting, Anna. I will keep the paper and tell Petka to call again. Happen the master or Yasha will be in.' She stooped, pushed the heavy brown-bound Latin book towards me, and smiled.

'Dry your eyes, little one. I reckon that is where your heart is.' She glanced at my bethumbed Tacitus and went.

I think Agasha must have spoken to my father. From that day on, whatever bills came to Khlébnikovs were dealt with by the two clerks. To my delight, the detestable slate, sponge and stocks of chalk vanished from the study room.

Monsieur Allion and others still frequented Khlébnikovs. There were two newcomers. Herr Krause, an inhabitant of the German Quarter and a native of Stettin, instructed me in German, geography and 'the affairs of the world'. I liked him. A plump, rosy-cheeked man in a neat grey wig, a tidy green coat and fawn smalls, Herr Krause was devoted to his native city and never lost a chance of reminding me that our Tsarina was born at Stettin. Herr Krause suggested a prosperous grocer rather than a tutor, but he taught well. He stirred my interest in geography until the names of countries, mountains, rivers and cities became living identities to me. At the usual interval when a white-coifed maid brought in the refreshments, Herr Krause would say every day— of course in German:

'Ah Fraülein Anna, you are indeed fortunate in having such an enlightened father.'

I was indifferent to food, but it pleased me to see Herr Krause enjoy his lavishly buttered *kalách*.

The second newcomer came once a week, and soon enough became a weekly penance. His name was Luka Petrovich Andreev, and he worked somewhere as a clerk. He wore 'German' clothes, but they sat oddly on his ungainly bulky body. On entering the room, he would at first cross himself, then prostrate twice in front of the icon in the corner, cross himself again, and then turn towards me, his plump face reflecting sympathy rather than welcome so that I felt my Aunt Xenia would have approved of him.

Andreev came to instruct me in Russian language, history and literature. He droned like an overworked subdeacon, and I never knew how my father had come to engage him. Andreev did not teach: he preached, and he preached badly. I loathed him but I would not say so to my father.

When the refreshment interval came, Andreev rose. He did not thank the girl, but he turned towards the icon, crossed himself two or three times, and mumbled a long prayer of thanksgiving to 'the Giver of all'. His devotions done he would sit down and examine the tray. On one occasion he said:

'*Báryshna, báryshna*, I am sorry—but here is a little fish fried in butter and they have brought milk, too.'

'Well?' I asked coldly.

'But—but—' he stammered, his rosy cheeks turning red, 'it is a vigil today.'

I leant over the tray.

'Well, Luka Petrovich, eat the bread and drink your tea.' I added maliciously, 'I had an idea that vigils did not start till the evening.'

'Ah! I forgot! God be merciful to all sinners,' mumbled Andreev and attacked the prohibited fish with gusto.

Soon enough he and I had a battle royal over Peter the Great. Andreev was most punctilious and accurate about facts, but when it came to comment, my temper flared up.

'Yes,' I heard my teacher drone, 'he was a great Tsar, but he did not understand Russia.'

'Why?' I asked sweetly.

Andreev blushed.

'Well, you see, *báryshna*—'

'Don't call me that! I am a merchant's daughter. They christened me Anna!'

'Well, then, Anna, if I may take such a liberty, Tsar Peter trampled on so many ancient traditions.'

'They asked to be trampled on—' I broke in coolly. 'You have taught me some history, Luka Petrovich. Russia could not go on in her isolation. Why, abroad they thought her a barbarian country. Tsar Peter,' I cried exultantly, 'was glorious and great and brave.'

'He killed his own son, Anna.'

'That son, had he lived, would have turned Russia into old Muscovy,' I retorted. 'No, Luka Petrovich—don't run down Tsar Peter to me, I beg you. He made our country. Yes, he did.'

Andreev, having forgotten the vigil, finished the buttered *kalách*, folded his plump hands, and said silkenly:

'Now we stopped at the reign of Tsar Fedor, Tsar Alexis's successor.'

'Yes, a weakling of a Tsar,' I said abruptly. 'We had better turn to the ancient chronicles, Luka Petrovich, and I will tell the servants that you want tea and a rusk next week.'

'There are no vigils next week,' he mumbled.

I must have been difficult with all my teachers during those two years. To none among them could I even hint at my trouble. My father was so busy. Agasha and the others would not have understood. Girls of my own age in the German Quarter would have laughed at me, and the daughters of many merchants known to my father, avoided me: because of all the lessons I had, I was considered not to be a fish out of their own river.

It all had to do with Yasha. He was twenty at the time, and for some two or three years he and I had no longer shared lessons, so busy did my father keep him. I was slim but not too tall. Yasha, never broad of shoulder, overtopped my father by several inches. He still wore his grey shirt and white linen breeches in the summer, and changed into woollen clothes of the same cut during the wintry months. There was no sense of distance between us. I remained his 'little sister'. Whenever some leisure fell to our joint share, we still wandered about together, up and down the leafy banks of the Yanza, into the fragrant meadows far behind Khlébnikovs, searching for mushrooms, wild berries and field flowers. Sometimes we talked or sang. Sometimes we kept silent.

But oh dear! Yasha spent so little time at Khlébnikovs. My father did not chain him to a clerk's desk, or burden him with any of the Moscow business, but he sent Yasha to far-away places, usually to the south and west of Moscow, to bring back samples of seeds, to give orders here and there. Often enough Yasha would visit some ancient monastery or other and there bargain for a manuscript to add to my father's collection.

Yasha travelled in the manner of a well-to-do *koopchik*, i.e. a merchant's son. In the big yard at home he would help the men load and unload the carts, unharness the horses, rub and clean them, and see to their nosebags. Often he and Semka would clean out the stalls, heap the manure on the barrows, and empty them in a field beyond the wilderness. Horse-manure, the best of its kind, was greatly prized by the Moscow gardeners.

But for Yasha's frequent journeys there were many and varied preparations. He travelled post in a well-built coach drawn by four horses. The driver had a pistol and a short curved sword, known as *yatagan*, tucked into his belt. The postilion, who rode one of the horses, was also armed. Yasha had two assistants with him in the coach, and there was no lack of good weapons inside. At their feet they had a long bast hamper, containing the men's gear, and a brown leather *pogrebétz* packed with all sorts of pro-

visions since in those days inns sometimes provided nothing but hot water, thin cabbage soup, rye bread; and hay for the horses. Next to the *pogrebétz* lay Yasha's elegant leather valise, made at Hamburg and given to my father by a German friend of his. Papers and money Yasha had in a wallet sewn inside his coat, and he had his own case of pistols in front.

Tsarina Catherine, whom we call the Great Empress, had done much to lessen the lawlessness in the country. Roads were policed by men in her service who would shoot to kill, but brigandage continued, and Yasha's destination sometimes led him down the by-roads, fringed by thick forests where desperate highwaymen had their lairs. At the time I did not know much about it, but later I learned that few indeed were the journeys when the occupants of the Khlébnikovs coach did not have to use their weapons.

Spring and autumn became my favourite seasons. Spring floods and autumn mud made travelling impossible.

Yasha usually left at daybreak. We all gathered together in the *górnitza* and my father recited a short prayer for a safe journey and a happy return. Then he turned round, Yasha knelt for his blessing, kissed his hand, hugged me tight, smiled at everybody, and went. I did not cry but I always felt as though I had been plunged into icy water.

I was old enough to realize that my dear, dear brother was the heir of Khlébnikovs. Either Fekla or some other girl in our service

dropped broad hints that 'the young master' was of an age when a
bride must be sought for him. I listened. I said nothing to Agasha,
but I resented the idea of a sister-in-law coming to Khlébnikovs.
What would happen to me, I wondered?

Here I must explain that, though my father was one of the
most enlightened and best educated men in Moscow and had had
me extremely well educated—to the amazement, not to say
disapproval of his fellow merchants, yet he remained staunchly
loyal to the ancient traditions. A family was a unit sanctified and
held together by God's grace. Sons and daughters might not
marry where they pleased. Their wives and husbands were
chosen for them. My father, who was a scholar, knew at least six
languages, and spent all his leisure on his beloved books, was
horrified to hear that one Maria, daughter of a well-known
leather merchant in Moscow, had gone against her father's wishes
and eloped with the son of a Polish landowner.

'Not of our faith,' said my father, 'and without her father's
consent and blessing. Nothing but evil will come out of it.'

Supper finished, we sat in the *górnitza*. I drew a deep breath and
ventured:

'But, Father, if she loved him.'

'I was talking of marriage, little daughter, not of love. My
father chose the bride for me, God be thanked—she made an
excellent wife for me.' He added: 'She and I first met in the
church. We did not look at each other.'

I stared at him.

'Our parents arranged it. She brought a good dowry and we
were happy together. But it is time you were in bed, little
daughter.'

I ventured:

'You had me so well educated. I know there are girls round
about who think I am half a foreigner though I never wear
outlandish clothes. Father, you—you won't push me into
marriage.'

'As if I would.' He smiled warmly. 'But it is early days to think
of it.'

'I think,' I spoke with a gravity out of all accord with my age,
'that I don't want to get married at all. And I know you will
never make me go into a convent, Father. So you will have an old
maid of a daughter on your hands.'

'Well, I would not mind,' he laughed, and sent me off with his blessing. As I climbed the stairs I felt quietened but I wished I could tell him how I missed Yasha.

The autumn of 1783 was windy, muddy and wet, but to me it brought bliss. Yasha, having been to Kiev, Souzdal, Yaroslavl, and Kazan, came back to Khlébnikovs and stayed because no coach could have gone over the roads, so deep in mud were they. True I did not see much of him—such long hours did he spend with my father in the book-room. Yet there were the mealtimes—and the precious hour before supper Yasha shared with me, telling me all about his travels. I shuddered when he narrated his crossing of the Volga on a bitter windy day. Having left the coach on the west bank, he crossed the wide river in a hired boat to get to Kazan.

'A good craft she was, little sister, but oh, she bobbed up and down like a cockleshell. We all had our feet and legs soaked. I must say I was glad when she got across, but you see, Father wanted me to go to Kazan. I saw Tatars there, small humped people with yellow faces, narrow eyes and plaited hair.'

'And they did not try to kill you, Yasha?'

'Queen of heaven, their manner was as sweet as honey.'

I stared at the presents he brought from Kazan: a pair of narrow-toed green velvet shoes embroidered in silver thread, a crimson silk headscarf, and a necklet of square-cut turquoises.

'You are good, Yasha, but these things are much too grand for me.'

'Nothing could be, little sister.' Yasha stooped, kissed my cheek, and I felt I was in heaven.

'Did you run into any bandits?'

He shook his head.

'Not once this summer, little sister—but I did see a lot of misery.'

'Misery?'

'Yes. They had a dreadful drought near Yaroslavl, and people were hungry. I saw some eating grass and nettles and stripping the bark of the trees. I wanted to stop and empty the *pogrebétz*, but my men said there would not have been enough to share among so many, and we drove on. Little sister, I closed my eyes not to see those people.'

'But, Yasha, I have heard much about poor harvests. The government do all they can to help, don't they?'

'So they say,' Yasha replied rather sadly. 'But, little sister, ours is an enormous country. Help can't reach everyone,' and he stirred uneasily. 'I should not be saying such things to you. Now tell me what you have been doing.'

'I have started Greek with Herr Krause,' I said proudly, 'and Ivan's wife has been teaching me all about herbs, and they have a young sister at St. Praskovia's. Her voice is marvellous. A week ago I was at Vespers there and she sang "Hail, gentle light"! Oh, Yasha, I felt in heaven.'

'Good,' said Yasha, 'and here is our dear Fekla to set the table for supper.' He rose and stretched his arms. 'Fekla, Fekla, I hope there is a green goose and pork dumplings. I am starving.'

'A turkey.' Fekla dimpled and flushed. 'Sweet turnips and sour-cream pastries.'

'Famous,' said Yasha. 'Little sister, let us make for the yard and wash our hands. I know it is muddy but we can change our shoes and there will be a brush.'

The icy water over my hands and arms, I laughed.

'This is also heavenly, Yasha!'

'What is?'

'Having you at home.'

'You silly little sister.' Yasha tweaked my plaits and laughed. 'Now back you go and change your muddy shoes.'

Yet that blissful autumn did not last. The winter of 1783 marched in quickly and, before I knew where I was, Yasha was getting ready for another journey. This time I heard he would be going north, to St. Petersburg. I examined the map carefully: it seemed a good road through Tver and Bologoye, and St. Petersburg was the capital, full of marvels. They had a girls' boarding-school there called the Smolny, and a collection of pictures, statues and other wonders at a mansion called the Hermitage. Yasha was going to stay at Mr. Green's, an English merchant resident in St. Petersburg, and Yasha was very excited about the theatre and other entertainments. Somehow I did not feel broken-hearted when he left. St. Petersburg, I thought, would certainly be clear of footpads.

It was a wonderful winter. I liked to wake in the mornings,

snuggle under my fur-lined coverlet, and lie very still, admiring the intricate tracery of frozen snow-flakes on my little window. The wintry sun would break and strike myriads of golden lights from the snow. In the room, the square brick stove, stoked well with logs overnight, made it a pleasure to jump out of my little wooden bed. My father not permitting hot water in bedrooms, a maid would bring in a huge jug of icy cold water from the well in the yard. My skin glowed from top to toe. Dressed, my hair plaited, my bed made however unskilfully, and prayers said in front of my small icon corner, I would run down to the warm, cosy *górnitza*, ask my father's blessing and settle down to enjoy the frugal breakfast of hot milk and a *kalách*.

My father smiled but he seldom talked at meals. The meal over, he would vanish into the office for the morning session with his clerks. On one such morning I suddenly remembered that it was the post day. I even smiled at Agasha when she set me to hem a towel.

'Quite a time before you bury your nose in the books,' she said.

I loathed all manner of needlework. Yet that morning I took trouble over my stitches, my mind busy with St. Petersburg. Would Yasha see the Tsarina and men known as courtiers who wore velvet and lace and very high heels on their shoes? The Neva, I knew, was much wider than the Moskva, and the ice set so thick that sledges ran to and fro. We had a book at Khlébnikovs with maps and pictures, and I knew that Mr. Green's house stood in a narrow street near St. Samson's church on an island called Viborg Side. Mr. Green, I heard, was a master at a boys' military school, and I hoped he would realize that Yasha was an Orthodox and could not eat meat or drink milk on fast days. Our friends in the German Quarter were very good about such things, but St. Petersburg seemed so foreign, I thought, pricking my thumb with the needle so that a tiny blob of scarlet spread over a corner of the white linen towel.

'Now Agasha will scold,' I thought, sucking my thumb.

But Agasha did not scold that morning. She ran into the room, her face radiant.

'Anna, Anna, you are to go to the master's book-room. Never you mind Andreev! He can wait, surely.'

I leapt to my feet. The stained towel slipped onto the floor and neither of us noticed it.

'Come on,' Agasha urged. 'Child, we have had a courier from
St. Petersburg and—'

But I was out of the room.

I found my father at his big table, littered with books, papers,
and two parcels wrapped in thick pink paper.

'Little daughter, I have had letters from St. Petersburg. Yasha
sends you his greetings and two presents. He will be with us
come Christmas, God willing.'

I stared dumbly. We were at the end of November. Yasha, as I
knew, was to spend the whole winter in St. Petersburg? Had he
fallen out with Mr. Green? Or what—I clutched the edge of the
table.

'Sit you down,' my father smiled at me, 'and stop looking like a
rabbit chased by a fox. Well, I have had a most pleasant letter from
Mr. Green. He and his folk seem to think the world of Yasha.'

'And so they should,' I mumbled.

My father laughed.

'Well, I think you are right, Anna. And Mr. Green took
particular care to tell me that their cook never sent a roast goose
to table on our fast days. Yes, I thought that would please you,
little daughter. Now listen carefully. You know that for many
years I have been collecting books and manuscripts, and Yasha
has been of great help to me. Now I have a few agents abroad, but
two of them have been ill and I want them to return to Russia.'

I nodded.

'So Yasha will spend Christmas with us and then leave for
abroad. That, I reckon, will put his education to good use. I have
good men at Khlébnikovs to see to the business, but your brother
will never make a merchant, Anna.'

'How long will he be away?'

'Two years, I think. I want him to go to the German states,
England, France and, possibly, Italy—' He paused and stroked
his thick silken beard. I waited, my heart turned to ice. Yasha—
away for two whole years!

My father talked gently. He called me 'his little daughter,' but
I knew he was speaking to a grown-up person, and my anguish
for Yasha's absence was gradually drowned in the pride of being
taken into my father's confidence. He spread maps and plans for
me to see. I had thought that Khlébnikovs meant the house, the
yard, the kitchen-garden and the wilderness. In reality, my father's

property stretched much farther than Kolomna. There were acres upon acres of pasture and arable, woods, meadows, and woods again. My father's spatulate finger moved from one spot to another while my dear Khlébnikovs became a domain, a kingdom. 'It is all yours!' I exclaimed. 'And it is to be yours and Yasha's.' He smiled. 'Now, Anna, you are good at languages and geography, and I know you are good with the men. I want you, too, to be good with the land. Ivan and Efim'—he named one of the men I liked—'will tell you all you want to know. Most of the land is rented. They will explain it to you. You see, child, I want you to be at home at Khlébnikovs so that when Yasha is back again, he will find a helpmate.'

I put a forefinger on a spot on the sheet spread out on the table.

' "Praskino",' I read, ' "arable". It is now under winter wheat, I see.' I frowned. 'Next year it must lie fallow—and then we can have oats or rye.'

My father did not smile. But he seemed contented, and if I dared, I would have hugged him.

'Well, Anna, you have made a start. I don't want to tear you away from your books, but I did want you to know a bit more about Khlébnikovs. Oh dear, that master of yours must wonder what has become of you. Take your parcels, little one, and I shall see you at dinner.'

I gathered up the two parcels and I bowed to my father. Once out of the book-room, I scrambled up the steep narrow stairs and pushed open the door of my little bedroom. The parcels flung on the floor, I went and knelt by the window-sill. Yasha was coming back and would soon go away again to foreign countries, and stay away so long. I should have wept, but I did not. I, barely thirteen years old, had been taken into my father's confidence and not found wanting. 'Praskino, Praskino,' I repeated, 'quite a distance from Kolomna. I must learn that map by heart . . .' That morning, Andreev, fortified by a mug of strong, sweet tea, slices of wheaten bread, a piece of smoked pork and a large chunk of raisin cake, never saw me.

It was wrong of me to miss my lesson, but I could not help playing truant that morning. I had to be alone the deeper to delve into the riches fallen into my lap. My father, always calm, kind and strict, trusted me. He must have known I wanted to cry on being told about Yasha's going abroad, and I also knew he respected me for remaining dry-eyed. The reward lay in the opening of many doors into the Khlébnikovs heritage, a signal proof of his confidence in me.

My own world was very small. Except for occasional picnics, widely spaced visits to one or two friends in the German Quarter, and two or three annual fairs in the neighbourhood, there were no social occasions and I did not need them, my horizon being enclosed by my father, Yasha, Agasha and the day-to-day happenings at Khlébnikovs. Sometimes my father had other merchants to supper, but I was not summoned to the *górnitza*, and it was from Fekla or someone else that I heard about the twelve courses served and much wine drunk. The succulent kitchen details did not interest me very much.

I had always known that my father was wealthy, else he could hardly employ as many men as he did, but the map he had spread before me spelt an abundance beyond my powers of reckoning.

'I must not fail him,' I kept saying to myself, and I turned away from the window-sill, and unwrapped Yasha's parcels. One contained two pairs of obviously foreign gloves of soft white leather embroidered with pink silk. The other had an elegantly bound volume of Racine's tragedies. The gloves were far too grand for me, but Racine spoke to my mind and heart.

'Racine and Praskino!' I muttered. 'Pasture, arable and Shakespeare! Well, I suppose my father thinks I can manage it all. I must not fail him.'

Yasha's home-coming that December of 1783 was a festival. It fell on so frosty a day that we kept stamping our feet by the great gates as we watched for the coach to turn round the last bend on the Kolomna road. We were all there: my father, the household, all the men and their wives, and the huge shaggy sheepdogs which kept running and jumping over the snow gleaming rose-golden under the wintry sun. My father wore his thick fur-lined *shúba*, falling down to his ankles, fur boots and a sable cap with ear-flaps. Close to him I stood, wrapped in sheepkins and woollen shawls, thick felt *válenky* up to my knees and huge fur-lined gauntlets on my hands. Oh, the cold and the pleasure of the cold!

At last we heard the jingle of harness ringing silver-clear in the frosty air. Another moment, and there was my dear Yasha in an elegant yellow, fur-trimmed *polúshubok*, a round sable cap on his head, and his blue eyes shining like sapphires.

I stepped back from the gates, my feet firm on the hard snow. I wanted to cry and shout, but I kept very still.

Duty paid to my father and a kiss on my mouth, and then the crowd behind us had to have their due. Yasha began clapping shoulders, kissing cold cheeks and mouths, and exchanging pleasantries.

Presently, our heavy clothes shed, we were in the *górnitza*, the long table spread with a fine white cloth, the brick stove breathing forth its welcome warmth, and I heard Yasha laugh, that dear familiar laughter which brought back so much of our shared years.

'Queen of heaven! What a spread! Agasha dear, they did not starve me at Mr. Green's. All the same, it is good to see Moscow food! They never put an honest crisp *karaváy* on the table—just snippety wheaten rolls big enough for a flea!'

We laughed and plied him with the good things spread on the table. The cloth whisked off, my father and Yasha began filling their pipes.

'And did my little sister cry her eyes out when she heard about my leaving for foreign parts?'

'Never a tear,' replied my father comfortably. 'Anna has a head on her shoulders, for all she is years younger than you are, my son. But give me the news from the capital.'

Yasha crouched on the floor, his head thrown back.

'Well, the Tsarina is doing famously, and they all love her. Indeed, she is a great Catherine, Father.' He stopped. 'But here is something that will never be printed in a news-sheet. That son of hers is odd! Such fancies you would never imagine, Father! Why, the Grand-Duke thinks he will be either poisoned or disinherited, or just murdered in broad daylight! Poor Tsarina! She has got her grandchildren with her. That is not just market gossip either. The Grand-Duke and his wife live at Gatchina. I heard that people hardly ever see them at court. Now here is something which is a deadly secret.' Yasha lowered his voice. 'The Tsarina may disinherit him—so many think. The Grand-Duke could never govern. Now the Tsarina's eldest grandson, Alexander, gives fair promise. Rising seven he is now.'

My father looked grave.

'I have heard something and thought it mere gossip. But the Tsarina—God save her—is in her mid-fifties! You are right, Yasha, not a matter to shout about in a market-place. Well, did you see the elephants?'

'Just once! Oh, Anna, they are so enormous that a huge house had to be built for them, and yet so gentle a child could feed them and not get hurt. They are kept at the Tsarina's expense and a nice big hole they must make in her pocket, I reckon. A five-pound *karaváy* is a mere bite for them! And I saw a French play and a ballet and oh, a dance on the Neva—'

My father and I stared.

'Yes, on the ice. They all wore skates. I bought a ticket for a rouble and went down a wooden stairway by St. Isaac's bridge.

Mr. Green and I went together. No, we did not dance but just watched. What a crowd! Some holiday it must have been! There were bakers and booksellers, soldiers and soapmakers, all muffled up to their eyes—such a frosty morning! They danced foreign steps and "Russkáya" too, and a giant of a grenadier danced "Trepak" all on his own.'

'Oh, Yasha! Fancy! Dancing on the ice! And did you see the Tsarina?'

'Once, in an open sledge! Oh, Anna, she is lovely! I heard later she was on her way to the new almshouses on the Fontanka. She is good to the poor—good to everybody.' Yasha smiled at me.

'Heard of Poisier, little sister?'

I shook my head.

'Well, he is a court jeweller and he has a shop on Nevsky Prospect. I got something there—'

'Oh, Yasha! Not for me?'

'Of course not! For Fekla's blind grandmother,' he teased me.

My father puffed at his pipe.

'When you have done with elephants and jewellers, son, you might tell me if you did any of my business.'

'Father, I spent most of my time tramping up and down the capital . . . I have brought a case of books for your library. Holinshed's *Chronicle*, and Macchiavelli and a rare edition of Chancellor's *Travels in Russia*. Rather shabby and very dear, but I knew you wanted it. Oh, in an abbey library I saw a Latin manuscript of one Saxo, a Dane. The monks did not think much of it, and they were so poor they sold it quickly enough. But that is not all—' Yasha paused, and my father leant forward.

'You have brought enough treasures and to spare, son. Indeed, I must be in your debt!'

Yasha broke in:

'I have got you a fourteenth-century script of Nestor's *Chronicle*. I remembered you have searched for it for years and years. It cost dear and I had not enough, but Mr. Green lent me the money. I know you will send him the draft.'

My father gasped. 'Nestor's *Chronicle*! Oh, son! Why, it will be the jewel of the collection!'

'Father, let us call it the Khlébnikov manuscript,' I cried.

The case was already in the book-room, and I felt that, once the hempen cords were cut, my father would want to be alone with his treasures. Any book was not just a cherished possession to him but a friend. I drew Yasha away. Back in the *górnitza* he flung a small green velvet case at me and called out to Fekla to pick up the two bundles of presents for the household.

My own hands trembling, I snapped the clasp. Cushioned in crimson velvet lay an oval gold locket edged with tiny diamonds. In the middle was an 'A' in sapphires.

'Yasha, Yasha! That is far too grand for me!'

'Nothing could be, little sister,' he laughed and ran out of the *górnitza*.

What a very happy time it was! Days flew on wings. Christmas came ushered in with horrible blizzards, and we could not get to Mass that morning. Yet 1784 broke in a kindlier mood. Hardly a day passed but Yasha and I tramped over the fields and meadows held fast in their wintry sleep. Back at Khlébnikovs, we would huddle by the well-stoked stove and discuss the future and the details of his journey.

One morning towards the end of January 1784, Yasha left Khlébnikovs for Novgorod and Danzig. Ivan and Vashka went with him. Five postilions were to ride beside the coach. I knew that all the men, including the coachman, were armed.

We all met in the *górnitza*—my father leading us in prayer for a safe journey and its happy outcome. Kneeling behind him, I duly repeated the accustomed words, but my eyes were on Yasha. He wore clothes of the foreign cut: a green velvet coat, buckskin breeches and highly polished black boots, lace foaming at his throat and wrists. I knew that a fur-lined *shúba* was there for him in the hall and that he would be comfortable in the coach. I saw his face, the blue eyes collected but eager, and I prayed in my own clumsy way: 'Holy Mother of God, take care of my brother.'

The prayers finished, my father got up, and Yasha knelt for his blessing. We knew that Yasha had no wish to have a crowded send-off by the gates. He bent his head, kissed my father's hand, got up, kissed me, his eyes smiling, and I smiled back. He went.

All the little windows were so thickly crusted with ice that I could not see the coach leave . . . I turned. There was my father.

'What a welcome Yasha will get when he is back—'

'Yes, Father,' I replied quickly and ran out of the *górnitza*, scrambled up the stairs, and hid myself in my room. Presently, Agasha looked in.

'Tears are good for the soul,' she murmured. 'But, Anna, you had no breakfast. Come down, dear heart. The master would be happy to see you eat.'

'Agasha! Agasha!' I sobbed.

'Yes, I know, dear soul,' the roughened hand lay on my hand, 'but the harder the life, the greater God's mercy.'

So I dried my eyes, tidied my hair, and went down the stairs. The *górnitza* was warm. The table was spread with tea, hot *kaláchi*, butter and honey, and my father rose from his chair.

'You were good, Anna,' he said, and I did not want to cry any more.

5

A Battle in the Wilderness

Now it would never have happened if my father's sister, Mavra, had not as much passion for gossip as my Aunt Xenia for pilgrimages, prophecies and shrines.

Born in Moscow, Aunt Mavra had many friends among the local merchants' wives. Yet her visits were rare and I hardly remembered her. Married to a wealthy master butcher at Nijny-Novgorod on the Volga, she was now a widow and my father would have welcomed her often enough, but Aunt Mavra was convinced that all the highwaymen in the Empire were looking out for rich widows either to kidnap or to kill them. 'All right in a city,' she would say, 'not that I would venture to the market by myself, but on a high road! Queen of heaven! As to the inn-keepers, why, so many are in league with the brigands! Oh, Lord God, it is truly the end of the world! Look at my friend, poor widow Beleva—not that you could look at her today—heavenly kingdom being hers. She went to a little town, barely ten *versts* from Nijny and vanished! Not even a bone was found. Well, authorities brought it home to three devils. Swing they did! But my dear friend! Ah, God rest her with the saints!'

She spent Easter of 1784 at Khlébnikovs, but she would not have come except that my father, having ordered a vast quantity of corn from Nijny, had sent twenty men to guard both his sister and his goods.

I liked her at once. Small, plump, rosy, vivacious, and a chatterbox though she was, she endeared herself to the entire household by praising the furniture, the clothes anyone wore, the food, the way the house was run and, finally by the mountain of presents she brought.

'Now, brother,' she said one evening, 'there are many friends for me to see. I could hire a *kibítka*, but you will let me have one of your men, with a pistol, too, to sit next the driver—just in case anything untoward were to happen.'

My father laughed.

'Two or three men if you like, sister, and you don't hire a *kibítka*, either. But Moscow is not a country road.'

'You never can tell,' said Aunt Mavra gloomily.

The first time she went out, I certainly thought that she would attract any greedy highwayman. At Khlébnikovs, Aunt Mavra wore a brown woollen *kófta*, a plain skirt and rather clumsy low-heeled black shoes, not a touch of jewellery about her. She set out on her first journey in a resplendent pink satin *kófta*, its sleeves and collar embroidered with silver thread, and a dark green velvet kirtle. Her black kerchief was held in place by a diamond pin. All in all, she suggested a corner of a jeweller's counter. She returned, and entertained us at dinner with pieces of innocuous gossip about weddings, christenings, someone getting a stomach-ache after eating too many mushrooms, and someone else being cheated by a shoe-maker.

It was about a week later that, coming in after a stroll in the wilderness, I witnessed a most extraordinary scene. My father and his sister were in the *górnitza*, and Aunt Mavra's face looked as though she had been weeping.

'But do listen, brother! It is all over the city! Yasha is away and Anna is here. Brother, I have heard it in seven houses—everybody tells me the same thing. Anna is your co-heiress and she must be guarded. Elena Petrovna told me some of those men have an eye on her—to kidnap her, you know.'

'Now, now, Mavra, it is just gossip.' My father raised his head, saw me and smiled. 'Your aunt is certain you will be murdered, little daughter.'

I gasped. Aunt Mavra rubbed her eyes.

'It is not gossip, brother. You won't listen. Not only Elena Petrovna but all the others have told me the same thing. Anna is learning about your property, isn't she?'

'Yes, and a great help she is to me, sister, and she is never alone once out of the grounds. I send two men with her, and a dog too.'

Aunt Mavra shook her head.

'Sofia Ivanovna says that Prince Rostov's young daughter went to the Arbat to choose a canary, and she had a governess and three footmen with her, but the scoundrels got her just the same. A pearl necklace she wore!'

'Did Sofia Ivanovna see it herself?'

'No, brother, her cook's sister-in-law was there, and so frightened did she get, the cook's sister-in-law I mean, that she lost all her senses for a moment.'

'Now, Mavra, isn't that gossip? Prince Rostov does not live in Moscow. If he did, his daughter certainly would not go to the Arbat, three footmen or six—And here is Fekla coming to lay the cloth. It is a good dinner you need, sister.'

'And I shall enjoy it, brother,' poor Aunt Mavra said tearfully, 'but I beg of you take care of Anna.'

'I do,' replied my father.

The dishes were brought in and my appetite should have reassured Aunt Mavra, but she barely touched her food. When she and I were alone, I went and knelt by her chair.

'Aunt Mavra, you do believe in God's mercy, don't you?'

She was startled.

'Child, what a thing to ask! Of course I do.'

'Then, please, my dear aunt, remember that nothing is likely to happen to me. I always obey my father and I am never alone when out in the grounds.'

She kissed me.

'Yes, niece, I know you are a dutiful daughter, but Elena Petrovna does not gossip.'

I had no doubt that all those portly ladies sat round the *samovár*, drank tea with rusks and cherry jam, and gossiped to their hearts' content. Well-to-do merchants' wives, as I knew but too well, had far too much leisure. A little preserving and pickling, no housework, an occasional spell of needlework, church, taking food to prisons and almshouses, and endless tea-parties, the germ of any spicy story picked up from a cook or a yard porter. Nearly sixty years had flown since the death of Peter the Great, but the Muscovite merchantry still clung to the pre-reform customs and ideas. The men might or might not know their letters. The women did not. They all respected my father for his great wealth but they shook their heads on hearing that Yasha had gone abroad and that I, a merchant's daughter, had been taught foreign languages and 'other marvels'. Their husbands had dealings with foreigners but never broke bread under a foreign roof and Aunt Mavra's cronies shuddered at the idea that a woman should be seen at a theatre.

I knew many of them. Too kind to criticize my father in front of me and too honest to admire my so called 'accomplishments', they had little to say to me. Food, weather, the rising prices of wool and the latest robbery in Moscow, their imagination stretched no further. But all of them were women after Aunt Mavra's heart and I felt happy to think that the Moscow scene could offer her the entertainment she liked best.

On St. Peter's day in June we all went to the late Mass at the Donskoy monastery, came home and dined, Aunt Mavra alternately praising the monks' singing and the dishes brought to the table. That day there was an annual fair near the Dimitry Meadows some distance from Kolomna. The meal over, most of the household and others went off, Fekla promising to buy me some scarlet ribbon for a snood. My father went to see a friend of his in the German Quarter, and Aunt Mavra mounted the stairway to the guest-chamber, saying to Agasha: 'Just a short nap, dear soul. Ah, that sauce with the broiled chickens would have pleased an angel.'

It was a perfect day, and I made for my favourite spot at the bottom of the wilderness where about six old limes afforded most grateful shade. That year my father's 'Easter egg' to me was a handsomely bound edition of Shakespeare, and I meant to finish *Macbeth*.

Well, I was not meant to reach the last act.

The wilderness was surrounded by high spiked palings. There was no way into it except through the great kitchen-garden. My mind far away from Aunt Mavra's cronies and their gossip, I was about to turn the page when I heard muffled voices, looked up and saw three bedraggled strangers at the edge of the wilderness. Their beards ravelled, their dirty smocks having frayed hempen cords for belts, they looked like beggars, and Moscow teemed with them. I snapped the book shut and shouted:

'What are you doing here? Go back! Someone will give you alms at the back-door.'

The men did not answer but they moved forward and one of them leered at me. I did not like the leer. The man's right cheek was hideously scarred and his nose had red-brown pimples all over it. He grinned, and his rotten teeth disgusted me. The three stopped and stared at me.

It was a very warm day, but my hands were cold. In a flash I remembered that my father had given permission to most of the

men to go to the fair, and even if the men were at Khlébnikovs, no shout of mine would have reached the yard.

The scoundrels came nearer. Their rags stank. I wanted to shiver but I did not.

'What do you want?' I asked loudly.

The man leered again.

'Now, then, don't you start a pother! We mean no harm—but we are beggars and you are a wealthy man's daughter.' He shook his head.

I said steadily:

'If you want alms, go into the yard and one of my father's people will see to it.'

The three men laughed. To me, their laughter was as unpleasant as their appearance.

'See to it? Ay, and hand us over to the police for trespassing. It is not alms we are after, girl, it is you.'

What followed came in flashes of lightning. I remembered Aunt Mavra's hair-raising stories about kidnappers, demands for ransom and appalling threats, ruined underground cellars in the city suburbs, places teeming with toads, rats, spiders and deep in unspeakable filth. Quick on the heels of those stories came the resolve that the blackguards were to be foiled.

Now the wilderness ground was covered with scutch, with big cobble-stones lying here and there. One of them was close to my feet. I stooped, prised the stone out, leant forward and threw it at the leering man. The blow caught at one of his temples, he staggered and fell backwards, blood streaming down his face. The other two swore but they paid no attention to their comrade's mishap. They rushed towards me, their huge hairy fists clenched.

There was no other cobble near enough and I screamed wildly.

'Killed poor Petka, have you?' hissed one of the men and clutched my shoulder just as savage barking broke out from the kitchen-garden. Half-dead with fright, my eyes misty, I saw Tiger and Mylka, two of our biggest mastiffs, race across the wilderness. Tiger's jaws caught at one man's leg, Mylka pinned the other one down. The one called Petka still lay on the ground. Coward that I was, I closed my eyes.

When I came round, I found myself in bed in my little chamber. I felt very cold and was shaking from head to foot. A kitchen girl stood fussing over me, and my Aunt Mavra kept rubbing my forehead with vinegar.

'Queen of heaven be praised,' I heard the girl say huskily. 'Will you be wanting a cool drink?'

I shook my head. She stepped out of the room. Then I saw my Aunt Mavra fling herself down on a coffer and break into a flood of tears, her plump body shaking right and left. I said timidly:

'I am sorry I was such a fool to get frightened. But they did look nasty. Aunt Mavra, what are you crying for?'

She wiped her cheeks with the sleeve of her pink *kófta*, stared towards the window and said shakily:

'Thank all the saints that Semka and his wife did not go to the fair. They came out to cut the broad beans in the kitchen-garden, but the hounds heard you first.'

'Yes,' I said as patiently as I could, 'but why should you cry, Aunt Mavra? I am all right! I am afraid I did hit one of the men rather hard.'

Aunt Mavra gulped noisily.

'Why should I cry, Anna? Because it is my fault. I heard all the stories about kidnapping and such, and I told all my friends I was anxious for you, seeing you are my brother's only daughter, Yasha away and all, and it must have got about—' she wailed. 'Just think what might have happened to you.'

'But nothing did,' I muttered, 'except that I fear I killed one of them.'

'You did not kill him,' sniffed my aunt.

'Aunt Mavra, they said they were hungry. Did they get anything?'

'Get anything?' she echoed. 'They are locked up by now and it is the gallows for them, Anna.'

Later I heard the three men were hanged in Lobnoye Square. Those were cruel days and the law was harsh, but at the time my country teemed with brigands and vagabonds who did not care whether they maimed or killed anyone falling into their clutches. A man from Khlébnikovs went to watch the execution.

'They swung merrily,' he said on his return, and added, 'Hanging is far too good for such swine. They should have been broken on the wheel.'

The experience left its stamp on me. I was sorry for Aunt Mavra and sorry for the scoundrels whom I included in my prayers. I think Aunt Mavra never told my father about her gossiping and I kept her confidence. Agasha, horrified by my near escape, would follow me if I ventured as far as the kitchen-garden. My father, back from his visit at the German Quarter, merely said to me:

'Anna, when you go to the wilderness, take Tiger and Mylka with you,' and, the order given, he never again referred to the incident.

Nobody ever knew how those three men got into the wilderness, but Khlébnikovs was so spacious, and on that day most of the household had gone to the fair.

In my next letter to Yasha I never mentioned the episode, and
to this day I cannot tell if he ever heard about it from my father.
I knew that precautions were taken. Instead of the single night-
watchman we used to have, there were now three men, pistols
stuck into their belts, and the dogs kept them company. The men
would be stationed in the yard. My little casement faced it, and
one warm summer night I was awakened by extremely stentorian
snores. I listened, but the dogs kept quiet. In the morning I
laughed, telling Agasha about our guardians, but she did not
even smile.

'I shall see to it,' she said grimly, 'but don't you tell the master,
Anna. Ivan will settle it. That would have been Fedka, a bad
Easter to him. Drinks like a fish, he does, and treats others.
Many a time did I take him to task. If—heaven guard us, anything
untoward happened the master would have no mercy on Fedka!'

I stopped plaiting my hair.

'But there are our dogs.'

'Tiger is all right,' she replied, 'so well-trained he is that he
would not even sniff at anything offered him by a stranger, but
Mylka and the others—' she shrugged, 'why they would fight
each other for a scrap of meat—poison or no poison. Oh, Anna
dear, what a fool you have for your Nannie—to frighten you so!'

I flung my arms round her neck.

'No, no, Agasha, nothing can now frighten me.'

I could not explain it even to myself. It seemed as puzzling as
the multiplication table I had never mastered. I merely felt that
something had changed within me that June afternoon in the
wilderness, but I could fit no words to it. I muttered lamely:

'See, Agasha, when I say "Thou heavenly king, our comforter,"
I pray for those unfortunate men. They meant to hurt me, I
know, but oh dear, life was not very gentle with them. They
could not help it. But they were shriven and all before they died,
so I think things are well with them now.'

Agasha stared at me, her eyes wide.

'It is all your books, child. Why, they would have murdered
you. Now there is your Aunt Mavra clop-clopping down the
stairs. Go and have your breakfast, Anna.'

I went to the *górnitza*, greeted my father as he read Yasha's
latest letter, sent from somewhere in Germany, drank my milk and
ate a few *baránki*, but my mind was far away, and not even to my

wise confessor at the Donskoy monastery could I open my thoughts. I knew the gospel and I knew that Christ forgave everybody. But man made laws, and those laws had nothing to do with mercy. It seemed so very puzzling since we were a Christian country.

My Aunt Mavra was in high spirits that morning. Dressed in a coffee-coloured linen *kófta* and a green kirtle, with a turquoise necklace falling down her breast, she buttered her *kalách* and said:

'Why, I do call it generous of you, brother, to settle it all so comfortably. With all the men you are sending with me, I would snap my fingers at any highwaymen!' She bit into her *kalách* and smiled at me.

'Well, niece, would you like to see Nijny-Novgorod? It is a famous city, and what a fair!'

I had not expected the invitation and glanced at my father. He smiled.

'Perhaps next year, sister, and I will send Anna down by the Volga. She would like that. My Yasha will be back by then,' he paused. 'Anna helps me so much.'

'Let her come for Trinity Sunday,' cried my aunt. 'Why, Anna will be fifteen then! Time to look for a bridegroom for her!'

'It is for Anna to find him,' answered my father.

6

Another Adventure at Khlébnikovs

Some time in August my Aunt Mavra, assured by my father of a reliable escort, decided to brave all the perils of a return journey to Nijny-Novgorod. The day before she left, she took me with her on an excursion to the Kremlin where we visited several cathedrals, Aunt Mavra generous with her alms to beggars, and spending a prodigious sum of money on wax candles. We got back into the open *kibítka*, Aunt Mavra's anxious eyes darting right and left to see if any brigands were in sight. But the vast spaces of the Kremlin seemed quiet in their hallowed majesty. She wiped her cheeks with a pink silk handkerchief and grinned at me.

'Now I shall be able to assure most pious friends at Nijny that I have done my duty.' She sighed and added:

'Queen of heaven forgive me, but I don't hold with too much piety, Anna! I have always thought it was like adding salt to a well-pickled cucumber.'

We returned to Khlébnikovs some time before dinner. Aunt Mavra scrambled out of the *kibítka* and said over her shoulder:

'Come to my room, niece. I have something to say to you.'

But at first she had nothing to say. She tumbled into a little chair by the casement, pointed at a coffer, and said rather huskily:

'That is for you, Anna, to remember me by,' and closed her eyes. I guessed the August heat must have exhausted her.

Amazed, I knelt by the coffer. I had never had such riches bestowed on me. Two pairs of soft leather lilac slippers, a Persian shawl, a bolt of fine pink silk, a gold bracelet with a square ruby and a string of finely matched pearls! I kept murmuring:

'Aunt Mavra you should not, you should not. It is too much.'

She stirred and opened her eyes.

'Don't talk rubbish! I have no children. You are my niece—and I don't want any thanks. Now, Anna, I am a *koopchika* and was never taught my letters. I beg of you—don't marry a merchant—'

'Oh—'

'My dear brother,' said Aunt Mavra, 'was unlike any of us. It was always all books and learning with him, but just look at what he has made of the business. Truly, a giant of a man!' said Aunt Mavra, and repeated: '*Velikán*. By God's mercy, may Yasha go the same way. Good stuff in the lad, I must say. Where is he now?'

'In France.'

Aunt Mavra sighed.

'Ah well, all foreign parts are one to me, niece. Will that be the country where they killed the king a long while ago? Infidels!'

'No, no,' I broke in. 'That happened in England.'

'Ah!' said my aunt. 'Infidels all of them! Well, you know Yasha was nearly christened Tikhon, and we have a small St. Tikhon's monastery at Nijny. Not a Sunday do I go there but I light a fat candle and ask St. Tikhon to protect Yasha. I suppose he has gone after books and old scripts?'

'Yes, but there has been a very poor harvest in France, so Father tells me, and Yasha is selling corn, too.'

'I trust my brother will get his money. You never can tell with those foreigners! Well, Khlébnikovs stands by its trade, niece, but that is what I meant to say to you. I don't see you as a merchant's wife. And now I must get tidy for dinner. Not a fast day, is it? God be praised.'

It was neither fast nor vigil, and the serving girls were pleased to see my aunt enjoy her beetroot soup with sausages, stuffed veal and all the rest of it. My father entertained us by reading extracts from Yasha's letters which abounded with crisp descriptions of Parisian sights, but Aunt Mavra, folding her napkin, said severely:

'I trust they will pay you for the corn, brother. Look at poor Xenia's husband—God rest his soul. Sold two loads of good seasoned oak to some German or other and never saw a copper!'

'Did he tell you so, sister?'

Aunt Mavra flushed scarlet.

'No! I have heard of it in Moscow. Matriona Kuzmichna's yard porter being the uncle of—'

'Oh sister, sister! That road will take you back to Adam,' laughed my father. 'That dear Matriona has been known to turn back because a hare ran across a lane.'

'But that is a bad omen, brother. Why, a neighbour of ours thought nothing of it.'

'And what happened to her?'

'Choked herself on a plum-stone, poor soul, and all because of that hare,' Aunt Mavra replied solemnly and bit into an apple.

Illiteracy, gossip, superstition and all, I was sorry to see her leave Khlébnikovs. Yet she had said that she did not see me as a merchant's wife. That puzzled me. I knew the law of inheritance; I knew I would have a good dowry but Khlébnikovs would go to Yasha. I was well over fourteen, and in our circle girls were still betrothed by their parents at an earlier date. My father, however faithful to the old traditions, would, as I knew, never arrange my marriage in the old way.

Yet I remembered that merchants' daughters seldom if ever remained single. Should no such offer come their way, any convent would open its door to anyone with a dowry like mine. Most certainly I had no wish to be a nun. I knew far too much of their way of life. Long, weary hours spent standing in unheated chapels, thick black habits falling down to the ankles, clumsy square-toed boots, heavy black *klobúks* on their heads, meagre fare, total lack of any conversation unless it were 'spiritual', endless stories of hardihood in the past—in particular, the legend of a holy woman in the desert, a crust and an onion being her provender for years. 'But why was she holy?' I had asked once, only to be told that the lady had seen God's mother in glory, which to my wickedly questioning mind was no proof of holiness, but I kept such ideas to myself.

Meanwhile, I was learning much of my father's business. I copied ledger entries, wrote out orders and receipts, and was secretly proud of my neat penmanship. Yet it did not seem enough and the earlier enthusiasm for my father's concerns lost its bright edges. It no longer pleased me, while drinking coffee with my friends in the German Quarter, to recount my tentative excursions into the world of supply and demand. Once Mitzi Klaus, the flaxen-haired daughter of the German pastor, said impishly:

'You know, Anna, what with your languages and all, I think you will marry out of your station. A Dutchman or a Swede, perhaps.'

I put down my cup abruptly.

'The Swedes have so often been our enemies. The Dutch are dull and gross. They drink so hard.'

Mitzi blushed. Some of her male relations were not exactly

noted for their sobriety. Sophie Kroenberg and other girls I was friendly with had heavy drunkards for fathers and brothers.

'Your country people,' said Mitzi sharply, 'drink harder than any.'

'My father does not.'

'Others do.'

'Anyway,' I said, 'I'll never marry a foreigner.'

'Well, you are far too young to think of marriage,' retorted Mitzi.

I was fond of her. We did not quarrel. She offered me another slice of cinnamon cake and admired the clear blue beads a cousin had sent me from Novgorod. In my turn, I praised her stitchery: she was making a fine linen cloth for her mother.

It was on that day in August 1784 that I made a discovery: for all my knowledge of languages and my interest in foreign countries, I was Russian to the very last drop of my blood. My Aunt Xenia and other relations had once amused me by their exaggerated piety, but Khlébnikovs had its roots deep in Russian soil. It had a peculiar smell I would never have found in the houses of my foreign friends: a smell of wax, herbs, lavender, incense. And there was much more. All our habits had Russian roots. My father could send his son abroad and bury himself in French and German books, but he took it for granted that neither meat nor milk appeared in the *górnitza* on fast days. Himself indifferent to food, he expected to find the traditional Easter night supper on his table. His religious observance was never exaggerated and always rang true.

The discovery, as it were, settled me down. 'You are born in Moscow,' I said to myself, 'and you are a true-bred Russian. Nothing else matters.'

On my way back from Mitzi's, I asked Semka, who was driving the cart, to halt at St. Praskovia's. He reined in. I went under the humpy porch into the church and bought a large wax candle to burn in front of an icon. It was no gesture of piety. I said no prayers, but I left the little dim church with the consciousness of having, as it were, put my signature to the discovery. I was Russian; there I belonged and, whatever my future was to bring, I could not be anything else.

At Khlébnikovs Agasha met me, and she looked cross. There was a towel I had been embroidering for months and she had just found it stuck behind the chest in my room, the fair white linen dusty and crumpled.

'I shall wash it myself, Agasha,' I cried, but she did not smile.

'There are two shifts of yours to mend, too. Queen of heaven, Anna, you are getting a big girl, you should be tidy about your clothes, but that nose of yours is always buried in books.'

'I try and help my father a little, Agasha, now that Yasha is away.'

'Not all that much,' she broke in. 'No, Anna, you can't make a meat pie out of a pike.'

And she added that I was not to go to the *górnitza* for dinner.

'The master is having company today, and he forgot to say anything till this morning. They are all off their feet in the kitchens. Six guests are coming. Fekla and I have been fetching bottles from the cellar, and the silver plate is out. So the master ordered. I said nothing, but I thought, "Wooden platters would be good enough for them".'

'And who are the guests?'

Agasha mentioned five names and added:

'Ah, and there is Pável Ivanovich Lukin.'

I curved my lips in disgust.

'Why must my father invite him? He is sure to get drunk.'

Agasha nodded.

'Of course he will, little one. The last time he came, they carried him out—so far gone he was.' She sighed. 'But it is the same with all merchants—they drink hard.'

'My father does not.' I stamped my foot.

'That he does not,' agreed Agasha. 'Now go and see to your sewing, Anna, and Fekla will bring your meal to you.'

Eyes blazing, I went to my room.

Now and again, as I knew well, my father entertained his fellow merchants. They came without their wives and I was banned from the *górnitza*. But I hated Lukin, a wealthy butcher from Khramóvniki, a gross man with narrow slits for eyes and pimples all over his face. I knew that he maltreated his wife and children and was brutal to the men who served him. I had met him twice and recoiled from the unpleasant leer in his small eyes. His huge red hand looked like a joint of beef sold in one of his shops, and I always thought that, if he were not so big, he might look like a leg of pork. But Lukin was no nonentity in Moscow. He had a row of shops in the Okhotny Road, some land to the south of the city, and a huge timbered house in the Prechistenskaya. I had heard people praise him for his generosity to almshouses, hospitals and monasteries. I also knew that he had one son and four daughters. I loathed him.

Fekla tripped in with my food and a budget of home gossip. She was sorry to be late but there were eight courses to serve and they were nearly demented in the kitchens. Creamed *bortch*, stuffed pike, a dish of kidneys in mushroom sauce . . . Here I broke in:

'That will do, Fekla. They will want you downstairs.'

It did not stop her.

'Twenty bottles Agasha and I fetched from the cellars! It looks as though twenty more will be needed.'

'That will do, Fekla,' I said again, and turned my back on her.

It was late in the afternoon when my father sent for me. I found him in his book-room. He wasted no time on any preliminaries.

'My friend Lukin dined here. He was the last to leave. He asked if I would consent to a betrothal between you and his son Fedor.'

My hands were trembling, but I said nothing.

'I refused, saying you were far too young,' went on my father. 'He is one of the most important merchants in Moscow and I can't ignore him, but I can't see my only daughter betrothed to a drunkard's son. Anna, was I right?'

I felt dumb. I nodded.

'Well, then, get back to your books.' He added dryly, 'For once Lukin was sober enough to speak clearly and to walk out of the house.'

I leapt forward, knelt by him, and covered his hands with my kisses.

'Now then, now then, Anna,' he said swiftly, 'did you imagine I could have such a sot's brat for my son-in-law?'

'No, no, no,' I gulped. 'Father, I do loathe him and that Fedor of his is such a fool.'

'He is,' agreed my father, 'for all he is a master butcher's son, he could not tell one joint from another. Why, I've heard folks say that Fedor Lukin could not tell mutton from pork.'

We both laughed, and I went off to wash the dirty towel and to

finish mending my shifts. At supper that evening I won a smile
from Agasha.

Some time later, a day opened in one of those still and golden
August mornings which, as Yasha told me, could be seen nowhere
except in the North. The sky was blue but it did not dazzle. The
warmth soothed but did not stifle. Here and there a streak of faint
yellow lay upon the leafage, but when the wind stirred them, not
a single leaf fell on the ground. It was a day meant not so much
for singing and dancing as for peace in the mind.

My morning's stint done, I made for the wilderness, my two
friends close to me, rather lazily twitching their huge tails. I wore
a sadly crumpled grey cotton *sarafán* and a blue kirtle. My legs
were bare and my feet unshod. I reached the old limes at the end
and sprawled on the grass. Tiger and Mylka, sure that there
were no undesirable strangers about, went to sleep, their shaggy
heads on two huge forepaws.

In a few moments, however, Tiger stirred. So did Mylka.
There was nobody to see, nothing to hear, and the dogs did not
growl. Yet both sprinted forward and I followed them. Tails up,
ears back, Tiger and Mylka panted through the kitchen-garden
and halted by the edge of the great yard. I saw the gates flung
open and quite a dozen of our men crowding round about. Beyond,
I saw a splendid crimson and black coach harnessed to six
bays. There were men in unfamiliar livery fussing round about
it.

I curled my lip.

'Some gentry or other! I suppose a wheel has come off,' I
thought, slipped into my tiny study through a back-door, and
started on a letter to Yasha, when the door opened so suddenly
that the quill fell out of my hand.

It was my father and a bewildered Agasha behind him.

'I thought you would be here. Come at once, little daughter.'

'Master,' Agasha's voice murmured in agony, 'how can she?
Clothes all crumpled and that nasty ink on her cheek! Let me put
her to rights, master.'

'It does not matter what she looks like,' answered my father,
seized me by the hand, and led me to the book-room. There, in
his own chair, sat a plump, elderly woman, her hair unpowdered
her plain grey gown setting off one of the loveliest faces I had

ever seen. My father let go my hand. I stood by the doorway and stared at the visitor.

'This is my daughter, Your Majesty. Anna, come and pay homage to our gracious Tsarina.'

I moved. I had no idea how homage was paid. The Tsarina at Khlébnikovs! So lovely and simple, too, without any frightening golden crown and purple robes. And yet what grandeur! Knowing nothing about homage I came nearer, knelt and kissed the small white hand. The Tsarina's voice rang like music.

'Get up, child! Why, what a scholar you must be! Ink even on your face! Well, you need not blush so. I do, too—' The Tsarina turned to my father.

'Well, Piotr Mikhaylovich, what a happy chance that one of my horses should have cast a shoe just here! I saw your house and a window with books piled up! So I asked about you. And they said you were a corn merchant. "A corn merchant," said I to myself, "and he reads German and Latin books!" So I had to come in—all dusty and in my travelling clothes! Of course, I have heard of you—you collect all kinds of rare books, don't you? And so does your daughter, eh?'

'She is too young, gracious Tsarina, but I have had her tutored.'

Here the door behind me opened a little and my father backed, took a tray, and knelt, offering it to the Empress. Dishes, plates and goblets were all silver.

'If Your Majesty will honour me.'

'The honour is mine,' she smiled.

Fascinated, I watched those delicate small hands butter a slice of rye bread and fill a goblet with raspberry water. As the Empress ate and drank, I felt myself to be drawn into the very heart of a dream.

'How old is your daughter?'

'Fourteen, gracious Tsarina. I have had her tutored at home. She knows four languages.'

The Empress shot a glance at me.

'And which do you like best, child?' she asked in French.

Instinctively I answered in the same language.

'English, ma'am, German and Latin, too.'

'Why, you are far more learned than I am,' smiled the Empress, her small even teeth gleaming like pearls. From a purple velvet reticule she brought out a gold buckle with her initial in diamonds. 'Here is a trifle to remind you of our first meeting, child.'

Cheeks burning, I knelt to receive the gift, kissed the Empress's hand, and murmured in Russian:

'Gracious Tsarina, I do thank you, and I shall remember this happy day all my life.'

'Prettily said.' She waved her hand and I guessed I was being dismissed. I got up, bowed low from the hips, backed to the door and made for my bedroom, the buckle cupped in both hands. I laid my treasure down and knelt before it. A present from the Empress! I knew I would have treasured a discarded glove of hers.

Khlébnikovs' walls were stoutly built and not a sound came from the book-room, but by excited chatter in the yard I guessed the Tsarina was still in the house. I saw Agasha, leant out of the casement and beckoned to her and Fekla. When they came, they gasped at the golden buckle.

'The Tsarina gave it to me.'

'And was she all covered with diamonds and pearls?' asked Fekla, her eyes like twin saucers.

'Indeed no! Not a jewel did I see on her. She took the buckle out of her bag.'

'And she talked to you?'

I nodded.

'Now be quiet, Fekla,' Agasha broke in. 'Oh, Anna! The Tsarina coming to Khlébnikovs and you, the master's daughter, just like a peasant wench! That kirtle is fit for the wash-tub, and your feet bare! What a disgrace! But the master would not listen to me!'

'The Tsarina never noticed my clothes,' I retorted. 'Her own skirts were all crumpled, and she said she often had ink on her face.'

Fekla started prattling again.

'The men say in the yard it is going to be a festival for us all tomorrow, and all the silver served to the Tsarina is never to be used again and—'

'Be quiet,' said Agasha again. 'It is a good birching you need and not a holiday. Now fetch some warm water and I will set Anna to rights.'

'Please don't fuss, Agasha! I feel I could dance all over Moscow and back again—'

'You look mad enough for it,' muttered Agasha when Fekla had gone. 'Now, tell me, child—seeing I had nothing but a glimpse of her, what is she like?'

'Every inch a Tsarina! Kind and gracious—but you never forget who she is.'

Agasha kept shaking her head.

'A great Tsarina she is and no mistake, but I have heard folk say she had neither a spare shift nor a pair of sheets when she came here from some foreign parts.'

'Well, she is truly Russian and Orthodox, Agasha. She made the sign of the cross before eating and her language is as pure as my father's.'

'You never! Stand still, Anna, and I'll give you a good scrub!
Oh, Queen of heaven, ink on your face and all!'

I believe the Tsarina stayed with my father for about an hour.
I kept to my room, but through the wide-open casement I
heard our men's cheers and the rumbling of the coach as it drove
off to Kolomensky Palace. It was long past our dinner-hour but
I could not think of food. The festival seemed to have started:
our people were dancing in the yard.

The Tsarina had been to Khlébnikovs.

I left my room and peeped into the book-room. The floor was
littered with books, manuscripts and maps. I turned to the
górnitza. My father was sitting by the brick stove, his long pipe
in his hand.

'Anna, you must be famished!'

'What a golden day, Father!'

'Our gracious Tsarina,' he smiled, 'is a most enlightened lady.'

7

I Become a Lady

The festival was over and Khlébnikovs slipped back into its routine. The silver service used by the Tsarina was carefully washed and locked up in a chest. My precious buckle, put into a leather case, found a home in my father's strong iron box. The golden August moved into a wet and murky September. The women were busily shaking and dusting winter clothes. At the end of October the rain changed to sleet, and nobody went out barefooted. The men got the big sledge out of its shed. Tiger and Mylka, denied their drowsy hours in the wilderness, sought comfort in mounds of warm fragrant hay at the back of the stables. My own cotton clothes changed for woollens, I went on with the accustomed tasks.

Everything appeared the same, but I had a feeling that nothing was as it had been. My father told me about his conversation with the Tsarina, her lively interest in all his treasures, her pleasure in finding a merchant to be a scholar, her gracious acceptance of some ancient manuscripts from a Kiev abbey and a few rare foreign books on Russia. These, packed into wadding and thick linen, were dispatched to St. Petersburg with a courier. Someone at court acknowledged the safe arrival of the crate, but at the bottom of the sheet was a postscript in the Empress's own hand: 'That mishap at Kolomna brought me great pleasure and profit. Catherine.'

I remember there were tears in my father's eyes when the paper, sealed with the imperial eagle, came to Khlébnikovs. He ordered a mahogany frame to be made for it, had it glazed, and with his own hands hung it above the lintel.

Naturally, the neighbourhood talked of little else for a long time, and soon enough fantasy gained over facts. A fishmonger's wife in the district was certain she had seen the Tsarina, 'in a gold crown and diamonds as big as pigeon's eggs', enter the porch of Khlébnikovs. At the Kolomna market they argued that the

Empress had come to see my father to discuss relief for the peasants of some province, 'so Khlébnikovs won't now send any corn to our markets,' they decided, 'all of it is to go to the famine-stricken places.' A cobbler's wife won quite an audience by describing the Empress's footwear: slippers of pale blue satin with high scarlet heels studded all over with diamonds. 'Strike me dead but it is gospel truth, folks,' she kept repeating.

Fekla never failed to regale me with these pieces of gossip. All of it made me rather annoyed, and things were no better when I met Mitzi Klaus and other girls from the German Quarter. Mitz in particular wanted to know if the Tsarina would send me an invitation to a ball at Tsarskoe Seló.

I stared at her.

'Why should she? I expect she has forgotten all about us by now.'

'She was so kind to your father, Anna. Why, Emma says she dined at Khlébnikovs.'

'She did not dine. She had some raspberry water and one or two things to nibble.'

'But Emma says—'

I broke in rudely:

'Tell that Emma of yours to stop repeating market gossip.'

Mitzi pursed her lips.

'Emma never goes to market. Why, they had seven maids and three men at the house.'

I said rather feebly:

'Oh dear, I am sorry, Mitzi, but I would much rather not listen to gossip.'

'And I suppose your diamonds are also gossip, Anna. But our yard porter is cousin to one of your serving-woman, and he never tells lies.'

'Diamonds? Well I never—'

'Is it not true that the Empress took a diamond necklace off her neck and gave it to you?'

I heard and laughed till tears rolled down my cheeks.

'Now, listen, Mitzi. The Empress did not wear a single jewel. She gave me a golden buckle which has some diamonds. She wore none. The jewel came out of her bag. You can see it when you come again.'

Mitzi said wistfully:

'Well, shall I ever? Why, your place will be crowded with princes and counts my mother says. I daresay your father will buy a country mansion!'

I roared with laughter.

'A country mansion! My father is a merchant, and all his friends are the same. Heavens, I would be lost in a mansion!'

We kissed as warmly as ever, but that day I was glad to get back to Khlébnikovs. Its rooms were small and plainly furnished, but there was so much space outside. The streets and lanes of the German Quarter were narrow; the little timbered houses jostled one another. The Quarter was overcrowded. Monsieur Allion and his wife had just one narrow low-ceiled room for his studies, her cooking and their meals. Mitzi's bedchamber was a cupboard built into the wall. The gardens were just so many patches of ground used solely for vegetables. The Quarter was not squalid, but all too often you could smell the garbage from the Yanza and the hovels outside the foreign settlement.

I was tripping into the porch when Fekla met me, her eyes bulging and her cheeks crimson.

'Into the book-room with you. The master wants you, Anna, but Agasha says I must not call you Anna any more.'

'Now, Fekla, gossiping again.'

'In you go—' She hustled me towards the book-room and her roughened red hand on the door hasp, she bowed from the hips and ran.

I found my father seated at his table, one huge hand stroking his long beard. He looked up and smiled.

'You would be away from home when I wanted you,' he said mischievously.

'But, Father, you knew. I rode in a cart and Semka drove me. It is Mitzi Klaus's birthday. I had a small present for her and we drank coffee together—'

'Yes, yes, and I had a courier from St. Petersburg here.'

'Letters from Yasha?'

'Come and look,' he ordered.

Three sheets of parchment lay on the table, a huge red wax seal attached to each. I walked round and bent my head. The writing was most beautifully engrossed, and every sheet carried the world-famous signature: 'Catherine'. I tried to read and I could not.

'Father—'

'The gracious Tsarina had ennobled me,' he said. 'Here,' he pointed at the sheet, 'is what I would call a pack of nonsense, if it had not been signed by Her Majesty—all about my service to the country's literature. The second document defines my rank—a hereditary untitled gentleman, "*Potómstvenniy dvorianiń*", and the third sheet confirms that you and Yasha and your progeny will inherit it. Were you to marry a cattledrover, that rank will remain yours and descend to your children. Little daughter,' he got up and bowed, 'you have become a lady.'

I sprawled on the floor.

'Father, you must not bow to me. And, forgive me, but I can't take it in.'

'For one thing, Anna, I shall be exempt from quite a few taxes—'

Greatly daring, I broke in:

'But you won't leave Khlébnikovs, will you? And buy a country mansion and have princes and counts for friends.'

My father sat down.

'Of course I don't mean to leave Khlébnikovs. I was a merchant, and I am a merchant, Anna! Princes and counts! What rubbish! What, I ask, would you and I do in a country mansion?'

'You won't change your clothes or shave your beard?'

'Certainly not.' My father made a face. 'I may have to go to the Kremlin sometimes—that is all. I understand that I may choose my crest and motto. I think the crest had better be a sheaf of corn. I'll have it engraved on a ring—to be Yasha's one day. But, dear goodness, daughter, what about the motto?'

I thought for a moment and clapped my hands.

'I know it must be short! There are so many Latin ones—but yours must be in Old Slavonic. Father, what about "*nie khliebom edinym*", "not by bread alone".'

'I thought you would contrive something, little daughter. All those tutors of yours did not eat the bread of idleness.'

'Crest, motto and all, they will still call you master at Khlébnikovs?'

'Of course. What else should they call me?'

'Then why,' I burst out, cheeks flaming, 'did Fekla say that she must not call me "Anna" any more.'

'Because you are my daughter,' my father said sternly. 'And

you are not to belittle the Tsarina's generosity. You will be called
"*baryshna*" by the household.'

'But I have no wish to be a lady. I would not know what to do!
Why, Yasha told me that in St. Petersburg ladies paint their
faces, get their hair powdered and strut about in velvet and
brocades. Would you like to see me turned into some such doll?'

My father leant back in his big oaken chair.

'I would smack you good and hard if you painted your face and
powdered your hair,' he said. 'A lady, Anna, does not depend on
the fripperies she wears. Your dear mother, God rest her soul,
kept faithful to her *sarafán* and head kerchief and the Lord be my
witness, I could not have had a better woman for a wife. You
can get yourself a gown or two of German cut, there is enough
money for that, but no high-heeled slippers at Khlébnikovs,
please.'

I should have bowed and kissed his hand. Instead I hugged
him hard.

The time of the year did not allow for a festival supper to be
held in the yard. We had it in the kitchen, my father wearing his
best blue gown. All the men, women and children were there. I
sat at my father's right hand and wore my best pink *sarafán*, the
Empress's present pinned to my breast. Agasha and Fekla sat
next to me. The best wax candles illumined the long, narrow room.
The cook and her underlings had done marvels. Four long tables
set against a wall all but groaned under the profusion of hams,
pickled tongues, stuffed geese, pickled beets and cucumbers,
sweet turnips, sour-cream tarts and jams. Candlelight glimmered
over the jugs of home-brewed beer, barrels of mead and squat
flagons of raspberry wine. Grace said, the people fell to. With the
last crumb eaten and the last mug emptied, my father beckoned
to Agasha who jumped up and produced a large tray with three
foreign looking bottles on it and innumerable glasses. Unhurriedly,
Agasha moved from place to place, filling the glasses. When she
had finished, my father got up, pulled at his beard and cleared his
throat.

'Now, friends, because I will not call you servants, I want you
to drink the health of your gracious Tsarina.'

Hoarse voices rang in chorus, 'long may she live', glasses were
drained, and I found myself shepherded to the door.

'Let the folk enjoy themselves,' Agasha whispered. 'There are

two casks of beer and one of mead. But it is time you were in
bed.'

Drowsy and comfortable I muttered:

'They looked so happy—oh, Agasha—'

'Our lady guard you.' She stroked my hair and slipped out of
the room.

A blizzard raged over the city for the next few days. The yard
was feet deep in moist snow and men put on knee-high boots to
get the water from the well. Khlébnikovs was warm, rosy and
homely. Nobody dared to brave the weather, and I spent many a
happy hour writing a long letter to Yasha. 'When you get home,'
I finished, 'you will find yourself a gentleman.'

The blizzard wore itself out. The roads and lanes of Kolomna
were thickly carpeted with pure firm snow, and two couriers left
Khlébnikovs, the hooded sledge packed with valises and letters.
It was possible to walk across the Yanza: the knobbly blue ice
held. Yet I preferred to stay at home. Moments of leisure were
so rewarding. A little away from the wilderness stood a group of
stumpy firs. They were not particularly beautiful in the summer;
now they suggested so many brides veiled in silver from head to
foot. The brief wintry day ended in throwing roseate shafts up
and down the remote white walls of the Kremlin. Even the
humble patchily blue belfry of our little St. Praskovia's had a
touch of beauty and the turrets of the Donskoy monastery seemed
covered with gold. In our yard, two huge snowmen, built by the
men, had copper saucepans on their heads. They were called the
Tsar and Tsarina of winter.

Little by little I learned not to make a face on being addressed
as '*baryshna*'. Agasha alone, and that in private, called me Anna,
and the two clerks spoke to me as 'Anna Petrovna'.

My father kept me very busy that winter. Supposed to write a
fair hand, I was told to catalogue his immense library. He had
books in seven or eight languages. Among them were several
volumes in Italian. I found an Italian grammar and began teaching
myself. It was an honour to enjoy the freedom of the book-room.

Brought up in the strict old fashion, I did not start talking to
my father unless I had to ask a question connected with the
catalogue. He was no idle chatterer. But, on occasions, turning
over a page, I would look up, see him lay down his quill, and
turn his head towards me. Nothing was said, but that look was

a reward in itself: such a depth of affection lay in his eyes, and my own quill stayed idle.

'A nice pair of lazybones we are,' he once teased me. 'And how did you contrive to get ink across your forehead, Anna?'

I blushed, snatched at a handkerchief and rubbed hard.

'Now you'll get ink into your soup! Little daughter, what a fine hand you write and how untidy you are!'

'But I try my best, Father.'

'Then stop rubbing.' He picked up his quill and all was silence again.

What a paradise that room was—with my father in his chair, my work, the precious books and the light-shot memories of the Tsarina's visit. Into that paradise crept a serpent one fine December morning.

I believe I mentioned Lukin before.

I disliked him fiercely but he did not come to Khlébnikovs very often. He came in that morning, still in his huge *shúba*, lined with bearskin. My father got up and they kissed each other's cheeks in the old Russian fashion. Lukin took no notice of my bow.

'Welcome, Pável! A frosty morning, isn't it? Some hot tea?' My father stretched his hand towards the brass handbell.

'No, thanks, Piotr, or what do I call you now? Still in your long blue gown, I see. And I expected to find you in velvet and lace and buckled shoes.'

I heard and hated the man more fiercely than ever.

Having disposed his bulk in the nearest chair, Lukin plunged in.

'Now, Piotr, my wife's cousin from Tver is staying with us, and he and I have talked it over, him being in the same line of business as yours. Well, then, he would like to make you an offer.'

'For what?'

'Oh dear, your business, man. I tell you, Kuzma is a sound man—'

'But I am not selling,' said my father quietly.

Lukin all but jumped out of the chair.

'What are you saying? You must sell, shave off your beard and wear foreign clothes—' He gulped noisily.

'I am selling nothing, Pável. My father and his father before him dealt in corn and seeds. So do I. I am a merchant, Pável, and that is my last word.'

'But it is against the law,' gasped Lukin. 'The Tsarina having enobled you, you can't engage in trade.'

I heard and my heart thudded. Much as I loathed Lukin, he was right. I remembered reading somewhere about the latest codex. Some of it had puzzled me since princes, counts and big land-owners were known to send cattle, horses and farm produce to markets. I heard of a young dandy from St. Petersburg selling some land near Moscow to settle his gambling debts. Where, then, was the difference? I could not tell, but I knew Lukin had come in the hopes of making a good bargain. He panted as he heaved himself out of the chair.

'Well, Piotr?' he asked, his voice thickened with anger.

My father said quietly:

'When her gracious Majesty bestowed the honour on me, I

made bold to write and tell her that I was a merchant, and she has since answered me that it made no difference.'

Lukin's small eyes bulged.

'Well, Piotr, or should I say "your excellency", my brethern will have none of you, and the gentry will put you down as an upstart,' he sneered and turned to the door.

'God be with you,' said my father, but Lukin did not answer and vanished. My father sighed, settled down at his table and picked up his quill. I smothered my sobs as best I could, but he heard me, and leaning forward, stroked my head.

'Little Anna, I should have sent you away. Now go and get your face washed before dinner. I could not enjoy my food with that ink-splotched forehead across the table.'

'Father,' I mumbled, 'you—you won't let his wife's cousin have Khlébnikovs?'

'I don't intend anyone's cousin to have it,' he replied.

Reassured, I ran out of the book-room, and that was the last Khlébnikovs saw of Lukin. His threats came to be proved false. The merchants of Moscow remained proud of my father and loyal to him. So far as I knew, none among the gentry labelled him an upstart. The only news-sheet then printed in the city devoted one column to the description of his collection and another to his mercantile activities. I was more than satisfied. The household being illiterate, I read the articles aloud to Agasha and Fekla.

'Please tell it all to the others,' I begged, folding the flimsy sheets.

To my astonishment Fekla giggled, covering her mouth with the palm of her right hand. Agasha smoothed down her apron and said gravely:

'Tell them? But they know all about it! No more upright man has ever traded in Moscow.' She moistened her lips and went on: 'Ah—but few folks know everything. Not a bad harvest anywhere but the master sends carts and carts of corn to help the people. If the Empress had turned him into a prince, she would not have gone too far. Indeed, few princes do as much for people as the master does.'

I sent Fekla out of the room and hugged Agasha.

8

Oh Yasha! My Yasha!

Easter came late that year of 1785, so that snowdrops and greenery could be brought into the house. So mild was it that heavy coverlets, woollen shawls and kirtles, blue, purple, red, white and green, were strung out at one end of the yard for the usual spring airing. Wafts of warm air mingled with the scent of crushed almonds, vanilla and other spices from the kitchens where Vlassovna and her underlings were busily baking and broiling for the traditional Easter night supper, *razgovlénie*.

Ours was a strict household; the 'Great Fast', known as *Velikiy Post*, was observed down to the last detail. From the Pure Monday, its first day, until Easter night we lived on root-vegetable stews, dry bread, mashed apples without sugar, carrot pasties fried in oil, and extremely salt fish. Used to such a diet from early childhood, I just accepted it, though unsweetened tea was unpleasant and I preferred water. So did my father. The little world of Khlébnikovs kept the fast just as strictly, and I remember how once Agasha, seeing Fedka's very portly wife waddling across the yard, remarked good-naturedly:

'Come the Great Fast, Mashutka will drop some of her fat.'

From her I heard about the priest at St. Praskovia's and the monks at the Donskoy.

'That is the way to fast, Anna. Father Vassily has one meagre meal a day, and I hear the Donskoy monks live on dry bread and just one onion.'

I shuddered. She smiled.

'Well, the master knows you could not manage that, little chicken!'

The unsweetened tea and the salt fish notwithstanding, I loved the Great Fast, its quiet, the low ringing of the bells, the solemnity. At Khlébnikovs we lived as recluses. Few people came to see my father about his business. There was no entertainment. Morning and evening, however slushy the lane, we attended Lenten services at St. Praskovia's, and how fervently would I repeat the Great Fast prayer:

'Lord and Ruler of my life, the spirit of idleness, slandering, and anger remove from Thy servant, but the spirit of purity, patience and love give unto me. Oh my Lord and my King, grant me the grace to see my transgressions and never to condemn my neighbour. Blessed art Thou for ever and ever. Amen.' Such words made me deeply ashamed of my anger against Lukin, my frequent outbursts of temper, and my hasty judgements.

During Holy Week our entire household went to the Donskoy for confession and communion. On Good Friday we attended the service of Christ's burial at St. Praskovia's. So calm an evening was it that our candles did not flicker as we processed round the little old church. On Easter Eve our good Vlassovna came into her own. The great *Zaútrenia*, Easter night service, began at midnight, but Vlassovna got things going some time before dusk. Two carts were laden with gifts for Father Vassily, the deacon and St. Praskovia's sisters. Two other carts drove off to the Donskoy. Finally, Ivan himself loaded the Khlébnikovs cart, Vlassovna watching him as he spread a huge linen cloth over our own Easter supper since everything had to be blessed by the priest at the end of the service.

The church was dim and cold when we came in, and I was grateful to Agasha for throwing a woollen cloak over my silver embroidered *sarafán*. The long service started with the deacon reciting a series of litanies, the nuns' thin voices breaking in now and again. We all kept standing, a slim unlit wax candle held in the left hand. But presently the bells trembled into life, all the big candles and lampades flowered into flame, and our own little tapers were lit, the altar main gates were flung open, and there stood Father Vassily in white robes, chanting:

'Christ is risen! Alleluia!'

'Verily is He risen! Alleluia,' came the vociferous choral response.

The taper trembled in my hand as I exchanged the traditional triple kiss with my father and several neighbours. The glorious meaning of the great feast shone like a light and, were Lukin in that church, I would not have turned away from him, so happy did I feel. Father Vassily came out to bless the Easter fare brought by his flock. The choir sang: 'We worship Thy cross, Oh Lord, and we give glory to Thy Holy Resurrection,' and I stretched out my right hand. My father's strong fingers clasped it and he whispered:

'There will be such a surprise for you, Anna.'

At Khlébnikovs all was ready. The long kitchen, well scrubbed and made gay by garlands of greenery and snowdrops, was lit by dozens of tall candles. My father never invited 'outsiders' to the Easter supper. His two clerks and all the household workmen and their families were the guests. By each platter lay the traditional Easter egg painted red. The food was put out on a wide trestle stretching the whole length of a wall: bowls of steaming green pea soup, slices of hard-boiled egg floating on top, huge steaming hams, spiced with cloves and flanked by chopped cabbage fried in butter, rows of the famous Easter cakes *kulichi* and *bábi* stuffed with raisins and glazed with white sugar. Finally, the triumph of the Easter supper: *páskha*, a pyramid-shaped sweet cream cheese, flavoured with vanilla, crushed almonds and dried fruit, the letters 'X.V.' (*Khristos Voskrésse*, i.e. Christ is risen) delicately traced in pale pink sugar on every side. To our dear fat Vlassovna an Easter supper without a *páskha* would have been like an unsalted cucumber.

People began crowding in. Cries of 'Christ is risen' and 'Verily He is risen' rang on every side, and benches were pulled towards the long table. The great silver salt, shaped like a swan, stood in front of my father's cover. I glanced at mine and saw the red painted egg laid against the platter. 'So the surprise is not a parcel,' I thought and sat down to the first good meal in seven weeks. Mead, home-brewed beer, *kvas,* and raspberry water laced with French wine flowed freely, and singing started when two men, aided by Agasha and Fekla, carried the monumental *páskha* to the table. I was just about to dig the spoon into my portion when I heard voices outside. I glanced at my father and the spoon clattered on the flagged floor.

'I told you about the surprise.' He smiled at me.

In an instant, the entire household got up and shouted: 'Christ is risen, young master,' and the dear, clear voice shouted back— 'Verily He is risen.' Through the door Yasha came in, hurried towards my father, kissed his hand, and exchanged the triple Easter kiss with him and myself. That done, Yasha moved up and down the long table, kissing every man, woman and child three times according to custom.

Food forgotten, I felt in a mist. I heard my father give an order to Ivan, and I saw two or three men roll in a barrel of beer and another of mead. Then my father got up and so did I. We left the kitchen for the *górnitza*. There were some sweetmeats on the table, but I did not touch them. I waited for Yasha, and he came in.

He was Yasha, my own dear brother, and yet he was not Yasha. His powdered hair was brushed back and tied with a red ribbon and lace foamed at his throat and wrists. He wore a plum-coloured velvet coat, cut short at the waist, grey silk smalls, silk stockings and silver-buckled shoes. It was barely two years since he had gone and what a stranger he seemed, but still infinitely dear.

'Fancy wearing a brocade waistcoat! You look changed, Yasha.'

'You, too, little sister! But, Father, Anna should not be allowed to wear a *sarafán*.'

'And why not, son?'

'Well, seeing that the Tsarina ennobled you—'

My father reached for his pipe.

'The Tsarina ennobled my name, not the clothes on my back. A fine figure I would cut strutting about in foreign clothes. I wear the signet, and one day it will come to you, but I don't mean to part with my beard and the long gown. I am a merchant. It is different for you, Yasha. You have travelled and mixed with all kinds of foreigners. As to our little Anna, well, she will soon be sixteen. If French furbelows are to her taste, let her have them,' he laughed, 'and oh dear goodness, soon enough they will get as ink-stained as her *sarafán*. She has finished a catalogue and taught herself Italian,' he added, 'so you see what a scholar you have for a sister!'

I blushed.

'And see what masters you gave me, Father, and Yasha was the first.'

He jumped up and hugged me.

The entire household had gone to bed, but we sat on in the *górnitza*. The candles guttered, but the dawn began painting the walls roseate-grey. A horse neighed. We heard the familiar sound

of water being drawn up from the well, and we talked on, and
listened to Yasha telling about his travels in German and Italian
states, in the Low Countries, in France and in England. I drank
in every word. It was just like listening to a wonderful book
being read aloud but, as I crouched on the floor, my shoulders
against my father's knee, I had an odd feeling that the book had
a chapter written in cipher and that Yasha meant to keep it
ciphered for a time.

We had a good scolding from Agasha who marshalled me off
to my room.

'Now it is bed for you, Anna,' she said severely and drew the
curtains across the little casement. I grumbled that I was wide
awake and not at all tired, but I fell asleep almost before my head
lay on the flat pillow.

I woke at noon to find the *górnitza* turned into a huge fair stall.
Yasha's valises being unpacked, it was obvious that he had not
forgotten anyone at Khlébnikovs. All the men had belts of fine
English leather, the women—head kerchiefs of yellow, green and
red, the girls—silk ribbons for snoods. Agasha gasped at the fine
honey-coloured silk shawl fringed with gilt lace that Yasha had
bought for her in Florence. Vlassovana had one in blue edged with
silver, and Fekla wept copiously when she was given a broad sash
of crimson silk woven in Italy.

Our own turn came last. There were two crates of rare books
and manuscripts in four languages. Yasha teased me:

'Some more work for you, Anna! Will you ever finish that
catalogue?'

But my father looked grave.

'I never gave you enough money for such treasures.' He
stooped over an exquisite black-letter edition of the *Magdeburg
Chronicle*.

'Well,' Yasha replied a little too quickly, 'some are presents.'

'Presents?'

But here a clerk slipped into the *górnitza*. My father's signature
being wanted on an invoice, he went at once, and Yasha
whispered:

'Little sister, I did not want him to know. It was luck! The
right cards would turn up again and again.'

'Gambling.' I was horrified. 'You know Father hates it.'

Yasha shrugged.

'He need not be told, but you have not looked at your rubbish, Anna.'

My thoughts still uneasy, I stared at the green leather cases, each of a different size. One contained a small exquisitely enamelled globe on an ebony stand. A necklet of garnets was in the other, and the third case housed a finely made casket of some strange pale wood. Yasha raised the lid and I saw three small gold-lidded crystal boxes. I laughed, cried, and laughed again.

'Oh, Yasha! Yasha!'

'Well, I saw these in Paris and thought they might please you.'

All speech gone, I hugged and kissed him, and forgot my unease about his 'luck'.

Days flew on wings. My brother, his grand clothes discarded for a grey shirt and white linen breeches, grafted himself into the household routine, working in the store-rooms, driving to markets, attending Mass at St. Praskovia's. He called on many old friends and went on long walks with me whenever we had leisure for it. He seemed the same, kind, open-hearted Yasha, but I could never get rid of the feeling that there was something that he kept back. There were evenings after our frugal supper in the *górnitza* when I would catch an unfamiliar look in Yasha's eyes, a look of longing and hunger. It seemed beyond my understanding. My father was so proud of him. Everyone at Khlébnikovs thought the world of him. To me, he remained a dearly loved brother, a close companion, a sharer of all my little joys and griefs.

I think it happened in late May. There was an arbour at the end of the kitchen-garden, a sheltered place furnished with a rustic bench and a table. A girl brought tea and some saffron cakes. I was just about to pour the tea into the large blue cups when I heard my father say:

'Come early June, Yasha, I want you to go South and get orders for corn. The spring was kind. The harvest should be good.'

Yasha's shirt was grey. Suddenly his face went grey and he twitched his lips.

'I am sorry, Father, but I have to leave Khlébnikovs at the end of the month.'

A pause fell. I heard the rustling of lime leaves overhead. My hands trembling, I managed to fill the large blue cups.

'A cake, Yasha?'

He did not answer. I glanced at my father. One hand stirring his tea, he looked down a long path fringed with raspberry canes.

'Why,' he asked quietly, 'must you leave Khlébnikovs at the end of the month? I have no wish for you to go abroad again. There is plenty of work for you in your country.'

I bent my head and heard Yasha's laboured breathing. The words he spoke were hammered out:

'I should have told you before . . . I must get back to England! I am betrothed—'

'Without your father's consent and blessing, son?'

'I—I—I,' Yasha faltered, 'well, I could not write . . . I meant—'

'Did you then think so little of your father as to imagine he would repulse a foreign bride?'

'Oh never!'

'Who is she?'

'A parson's daughter. She has four sisters. They are desperately poor. She is a governess. They don't think much of them in England, but they expect them to be gentlewomen '

'Well, she won't meet poverty here.'

Yasha did not reply.

'Where does she live?'

'In the North. In Lancashire.'

'Is there an Orthodox church near there?'

'No. There is a chapel at our embassy in London. But—but—you see, Father, she won't leave England—'

'Don't shake like an aspen leaf, son. You wish to go to England and marry her? I see . . . But what would you live on? I have never been abroad, but I fancy foreign beggars would not be welcome anywhere.'

'I can teach languages.'

My father looked at Yasha gravely.

'So you will turn your back on your people, your country and your faith, too?'

'But I love Caroline,' Yasha burst out fiercely.

'Listen, son. I could write to St. Petersburg and ask Her Majesty to have you refused passports, and nobody would blame me for it. But I could not do it. It would be like pouring water through a sieve, to have an unwilling and rebellious son at Khlébnikovs! Why, it would be poison. You got yourself betrothed without my blessing and consent. Back home, you have not asked for either. Well, I give you both. Whatever hearth you choose for yourself abroad will stand on bricks of your own making. Folks would say that I should have turned you into a merchant. But my consent is conditional. You have made my daughter weep. You shall not make the household wail and wring their hands—'

'Father—'

'Let me finish,' he said, and never before had I heard such an iron note in my father's voice. 'You are to tell nobody at all. What I say about the matter is my own concern. You will leave for St. Petersburg tomorrow. I understand there are boats for England, and I prefer that you should not see either myself or Anna in the morning. The men will be told that I am sending you abroad. I shall see to the funds.'

Yasha kept silent. My father got up but did not tell me to come with him. I felt I was turned to stone. He was in his early fifties

but he walked down the lane like a man carrying a burden too
heavy for him. My tears gone, I watched him vanish into the big
yard. Then a cold hand, Yasha's hand, touched mine.

'Anna—you understand—'

I wrenched my fingers free and stared at him. He was not just
a stranger: he had turned into a changeling. I wanted to run away
but I could not move. He began speaking so fast that it was an
effort to follow him . . . He could not bring his bride to Russia.
She would be horrified by just everything. He had seen enough
cruelty and misery during his trips through the country. The
Tsarina was supposed to be an enlightened woman, but she had
turned millions of free Ukrainians into serfs, and all the arch-
bishops in the Empire praised her benevolence. Russia was as
savage a country as it had always been. Progress and learning
were but a veneer. St. Petersburg was a cesspool. Here, Yasha
checked himself and did not plunge into unsavoury details.

'I could not breathe here. Even if I were not to marry Caroline,
I could not live here. It is all humbug and pretence screened by
piety and superstitition.'

He went on talking, but I listened no longer. That unknown
Caroline, who had stolen his heart, did not matter. Russia did.
To the very marrow of my bones I belonged to my country. I
did not deny that there were ugly streaks across her breast, but
she was my mother, my nurse, my cradle, and Yasha's words were
so many wounds. And I had loved him so.

I turned towards him. Those earlier, blissfully shared years,
now torn to shreds, were still there. He was a changeling but
once he had been my beloved Yasha. Memories crowded in and
tears misted my eyes. I flung my arms round his shoulders,
kissed his mouth, cheeks, eyes, and ran away.

My father often supped by himself. I escaped to my room.
Fekla brought me some food. I kept my back to the door, but I
thanked the girl, forcing gaiety into my voice. Agasha would
have guessed, but Fekla did not see anything under her freckled
nose.

Sparrows and pigeons, chattering on the casement sill, enjoyed
my supper. Exhaustion sent me to sleep. I woke up late, remembered all the thorns woven into the day before, and listened.
The usual sounds came from the yard, and then I heard Kostia's
rough voice:

'And wasn't the young master in a hurry to get off?'

'It's no joke going to the capital,' answered someone, and Kostia went on:

'Strike me dead—but never have I seen the master up so early. Hair and beard brushed, too—'

Here Ivan cut in sharply:

'Stop your chatter and get on with the loading, wooden-pates you! What father would send his son on a long journey without a blessing. Look sharp, all of you.'

I buried my face in the pillow and I cried my eyes out until I heard the door creak and Agasha's roughened hand stroked my neck.

'Leave off, Anna,' she whispered. 'Tears would not spin a cobweb. Think of the master—'

I turned and stared at her.

'You know, Nannie?'

She nodded. I leapt out of bed, washed and dressed myself and made my way to the *górnitza*. My father and I did not break our fast in silence, but neither of us mentioned Yasha.

9

A Visitor at Khlébnikovs

Khlébnikovs was such a closely knit community that everybody knew about the rift. The men, who served my father so loyally, were not flunkeys versed in ingenuity and polished in speech and manner. They were rough, illiterate peasants but, having grown up among them, I came to appreciate their deeply rooted delicacy of feeling. They had comfort and to spare but they never offered it unasked, and in those days I would not ask it even from Agasha.

My brother's decision to settle abroad would certainly have grieved me. But his contempt and hatred for his own country killed something in me, and I had no words to explain it. I knew, liked and respected many foreigners. I had a passion for their languages. I admired those customs I observed in many a friend's house in the German Quarter. I yielded to none in echoing the homage my father paid to Western culture. But his long blue gown, his great beard, his unobtrusive piety, his acceptance of many old traditions, all these had sign-posted my own way since childhood. I was a Russian, Kolomna-born, all of me belonged to my country. Young as I was, I could follow Andreev's recitals of miseries in the country and get angry with all the examples of penury, injustice and graft, but I could not disown my country. Fat Madame Allion sighed and wished to return to France, but Monsieur Allion, in between teaching me French literature, told me more than once that things were far from well in the land of his birth, and I felt for him. I saw him as an exile. Yet, even in exile, both husband and wife followed the paths they had known in France, from a Latin Mass said by a French priest to the golden *brioches* (buns) made by Madame Allion. All the friends I had there, English, French, German and Dutch, remained faithful to their beginnings. To hear Mr. Glass's children malign England seemed as improbable as to listen to a bear muttering in human language.

Yasha's passionate and embittered monologue destroyed my

feeling for him. Russia meant nothing to him. My last kisses were those we give to our dear dead at the end of the burial service, and the tears in my own room were those shed at a requiem. When some time in the autumn my father called me to the book-room and read me a letter received from England, I listened carefully but all of it seemed to concern a stranger I had not met.

'So he is married,' said my father, 'and at the Orthodox chapel. May all go well with them.'

'Will you give the marriage supper to our people?' I asked woodenly.

'No! That would be awkward! They would want to drink the health of the bride and I have told them nothing. Moreover, he has changed his name. You know that "Khlebnik" means "baker" in English. So he is Mr. Baker now.' My father's voice was very quiet. He might have been asking me to make some extracts out of Holinshed's *Chronicle*. Yet I, who knew him so well, guessed at the desolation he could not put into words.

'Don't you fret, little one,' he went on, stroking my hair. 'There was no harm in Yasha falling in love with a foreigner. Remember that nothing happens unless God wills it to happen.'

I ventured shyly:

'Father, you will be sending drafts to England, won't you?'

'Could I let my son starve in an alien country? Well, little one, there is work to do. Rain or snow wait for no man's pleasure.' He made towards the door, turned and smiled. 'I hope, little daughter, to see you married to a Russian.'

'I'd rather marry nobody,' I replied and went to help Agasha in the linen-room.

In a way I could not then understand, my brother's earlier and frequent absences from Khlébnikovs must have made things easier for me. By the time winter came, I found myself taking pleasure in work, in sledge drives, in helping to build the snow-men in the yard, in reading aloud to my father after supper, in deciphering Aunt Mavra's infrequent letters from Nijny-Novgorod. They were written by some parish clerk, she being illiterate, on square sheets of rough grey paper, but the man faithfully put down whatever she said. The rising prices of wool marched alongside a pig who strayed into someone's house, the priest's wife had to dismiss a cook for oversalting the broth much too often, she, Aunt Mavra, was lucky to find bright green glass buttons at a market stall, a vagrant monk, having stolen a pair of boots, was beaten hard by the cobbler, and the chimney in the *górnitza* smoked hard enough to cure four hams, 'and I feed in the kitchen, dear and respected brother and remain your devoted sister Mavra, and come spring, I will look for an honest courier and send a gift to my niece. Dear and respected brother, kindly send your faithful Agasha to some grand shop in Moscow and find me a pair of soft red leather slippers. They can be sent down by boat and by that time I hope to have a Christian cook not to poison my stomach with oversalted cabbage. And I trust this may find you in a better state than I am, dear brother, sad widow that I am with great trouble in my stomach but quite happy all on account of the new green glass buttons.'

'Aunt Mavra is a treasure,' I said. 'When is she coming to Khlébnikovs again, Father? She will amuse everybody with her stories about the cook, the chimney and the pig. I wonder if it was her own pig?'

'She does keep a small farm and employs rather stupid folk to run it. I have told her so scores of times but what will you? That aunt of yours says that one man is a widower and the other weak in the head, and where would they be without her? So I suppose, a gate meant to be closed, stays open. Your aunt would befriend an orphan toad! I will write to her. Best for her to come by boat up the Volga once the hay crop is in. She has a bailiff of sorts. He has no more sense than an onion but he is an honest man.'

Yet, long before my aunt's arrival, something happened at Khlébnikovs.

About dinner-time, on a bitter and gusty day in March, I was in my room when Fekla opened the door, her mouth gaping and her eyes bulging.

'Am I wanted in the store-room, Fekla? I have sorted out the carrots.'

'The master, he says he wants to see you in the big room.'

I put down my needlework, made for the book-room, and nearly staggered back when I saw that my father had a visitor. I was certainly not dressed for an occasion! I had on a grey woollen smock and kirtle, thick worsted hose knitted by one of our women, and comfortable but clumsy shoes made by a Kolomna cobbler.

The door having creaked, my father and his guest saw me.

Between them, spread on the floor, lay a mass of odd looking brown bulbs. At least, I took them to be bulbs.

The stranger leapt to his feet. He was tall and slim, dressed in what I knew to be 'German' clothes, elegant but simple, made of pale grey cloth. He wore no jewellery. His hair, brushed off a high forehead, was unpowdered and his cuffs had no lace. Yet I guessed him to belong to 'the gentry', and I stiffened. He bowed and I acknowledged it in the old manner, folding my arms and bowing the head down to the breast.

'Here is my daughter, Anna, Dimitry Markovich. Anna, this is Dimitry Markovich Poltoratzky, and he has brought me something very interesting. Just you look at these tubers. What do you think they are?'

I came closer, looked, and shook my head.

'I would not know, Father. Are they flowers, or vegetables, or what?'

The stranger bared his teeth in a smile, his brown eyes looked mischievous, but he waited for my father to speak.

'They are called "*kartoffeln*" in German,' said my father. 'I have heard of them. It was Mr. Green in St. Petersburg who suggested that Dimitry Markovich should call here. Their culture will help our people, Anna. One such tuber will produce over twenty little ones.'

'Sometimes more, Piotr Mikhaylovich,' said the visitor.

'Well, yes! You clean them and you scrape the skin. Then you boil them, add some salt, and that is all.'

I stared from my father to the visitor, who was still smiling.

'But—but—' I stammered, when my father got up.

'Let us all go into the kitchen and show the tubers to Vlassovna. She can serve them with the capons—'

The young man smiled again.

'These tubers can be boiled, fried, or roasted—'

'Tell it to my wise cook!' broke in my father. 'But don't bewilder her with German words. "*Kartoffeln*". "Potatoes" in English! I expect it had best be "*kartóshka*" to the peasant.'

It proved the oddest morning call ever. The visitor swept up the brown coloured tubers into a napkin and we three processed to the kitchen where Vlassovna was busily making the batter for a pudding. Eyes staring, arms akimbo, she listened to my father, repeated the instructions, and said firmly:

'Yes, master, but not today. There is cabbage soup, stuffed pike and a green goose with turnips. No Christian could do more, master,' and she looked none too amiably at the visitor. 'Are they truly fit to eat?' she asked.

The dinner to cook and all did not prevent Vlassovna from plunging into a gruesome story about someone's niece who, wandering in a wood, had dug up a root, to her unknown but pleasant to taste. 'Chewed it at noon, master, and gave up the ghost at sundown, she did. The evil one must have planted it for fools like her. They said she looked all shrivelled and her face as dark as a blueberry, and—'

'Yes, yes, Vlassovna,' broke in my father. 'Now see to your goose and the rest of it. The gentleman is dining with us.'

'Queen of heaven! Is he indeed? Well, I will contrive some apple pancakes, master.'

We laughed when we got back to the book-room.

'Poor old Vlassovna! She looked as though she were expected to make a stew of oak twigs! Father, I am afraid they will never eat them in the kitchen.'

'It will take time,' agreed my father and turned to our guest. 'Didn't you say they first appeared in England?'

'Yes, over two hundred years ago. They were brought over from America. Then they spread on the Continent. They are cheap and nourishing. You plant them in March. They flower in May, sometimes earlier. In late June you dig them up. A good crop will last through the winter—provided the summer is not too wet. The damp rots them. I have a small manor not far from the Yanza, Piotr Mikhaylovich, but quite a lot of land goes with it. I mean to have three fields sown with potatoes. Peasants do need a change from turnips and carrots.'

'You think of the peasants, Dimitry Markovich—'

The thin, finely chiselled face flushed.

'Oh yes! They need care. I was fortunate to go to England last year and I brought back ploughs, harrows and other implements. My father let me have his lands in the Kaluga Province. It is my duty to see that the peasants are looked after—'

'Ploughs, harrows and potatoes,' murmured my father. 'A fair enough beginning.'

Three days later, Dimitry Markovich being again our guest, we were treated to a dish of potatoes. Fekla brought it before the soup. Vlassovna had done her best. The potatoes had been washed, peeled, par-boiled and sliced, fried in butter and sprinkled with salt. We liked them. The dish was emptied. My father looked mischievous as he rang the handbell.

'Fekla or someone will peep in to see if we are all shrivelled up,' he chuckled.

He was right. Fekla came on tiptoes, glanced at the emptied dish, and gasped.

'Are you—are you all right, master?' she stammered.

'We have enjoyed the potatoes. We are waiting for the next course, girl.'

'Yes, master—' and she ran.

My father chuckled again.

'Poor girl! She quite expected to find three corpses on the floor.'

How odd it was that such a very common article of our present-day diet should have opened so wide a door! To Dimitry Markovich potatoes were but a detail. His conversation soon turned into magic as I listened to him. To improve agricultural methods in Russia was but a first step. Good food, decent huts, clothes, enlightenment and, finally, liberty—such were some of his aims for the peasants on his lands. The manor in a Moscow suburb was not his whole property; on his coming of age he had been given a vast estate in the Province of Kaluga.

I had heard much about peasant suffering and penury from my brother, but Yasha had talked with anger and contempt, having resolved to run away from it all. Dimitry Markovich spoke of these miseries quietly enough but in the manner of someone whom all these shadows concerned most closely. He described the huts found in the Kaluga villages.

'They were not fit for pigs.'

'What did you do?' asked my father.

'I engaged some carpenters from Kaluga and I have now brought an Englishman with me, Mr. Jennings. He is down there now and we have plenty of timber and brick.'

My father said slowly:

'Yes, Dimitry Markovich, you can improve the housing conditions and the peasant diet, but you spoke of enlightenment. That means schools and it will be difficult. You mentioned liberty—but emancipation is against the law, my friend.'

The young man leapt to his feet.

'I know it is—now—but it can't last for ever and I hope that my son may see the end of it. As to teaching! Well, I have nine villages in the Province and I have seen their parish priests. They all agreed to teach the boys—to begin with.' He smiled a little sadly. 'Most neighbouring landowners won't like it, but I am resolved to go on.'

'More power to your elbow,' murmured my father.

'You see, Piotr Mikhaylovich, there is your cook. She is a peasant but not a serf, and yet she is a slave to every superstition inherited from her grandmother. I am a Russian to the backbone. Tradition stands for much, but oh—what a lot of useless superstitions crowd the way! And many are harmful. I stayed on the estate a few weeks ago, they told me that one of the horses had got the evil eye and must be killed. So I got hold of Mr. Jennings who has some knowledge of animal ailments. The poor horse had got a nail in his left fetlock! The evil eye indeed! All was well in the end,' he smiled, 'and that without any incantations whispered over the horse. You see what I mean. But one has to be cautious not to cut too sharply into peasant traditions.'

From the potato culture, properly built huts and animal ailments, the talk drifted into different channels. Dimitry Markovich spoke quietly, but his eyes looked starry.

'I am glad I have been abroad, but there is no place for a Russian to settle in. St. Petersburg is like Europe in little, and I could not live there. Look at France! They walk in jewelled shoes, eat delicately and dance at Versailles. In the countryside people are starving. There is much disquiet. I fear King Louis's days are numbered. England is industrious and prosperous, but there is trouble with her American colonies and her working people fare none too well. As to the German states,' he sighed. 'One Sunday I halted in a village in Wurtemberg and went into a farmhouse. Clean enough, but poor was not the word for it! Man, wife and nine children! The man over-taxed and down-trodden. Their Sunday dinner was half a sausage, two boiled potatoes and an onion. The woman told me they had sausages on Sunday only. Clean they were, but so shabby and thin! Yet not too far away stood a baron's castle where they feasted every day and drank French wine by the gallon. I stayed one night there. I said to the Baroness, "People are starving at your gates." "The poor," she laughed, "would not be happy unless they complained. Why, they have their sausages on Sundays. What more do they want?" Piotr Mikhaylovich, such things are all wrong.'

My father nodded.

'But there have always been people like you, Dimitry Markovich. By the way, where is that manor of yours near Moscow? Not far from the Yanza, you said.'

'It used to be my father's *podmoskóvnaya*. He used to stay there often enough, an Italian architect built the manor—small but elegant. My father had it made over to me when I came of age. My mother has never cared for Moscow. I often stay there, and I have a real treasure of a housekeeper. She used to be maid to my sister Elizabeth. I hope that some day she will leave Lobchino and come to Kaluga. She is sterling, my dear old Akimovna!'

I stirred.

'Her Christian name is Mavra and she looks so kind. And there is a room all sapphire velvet and mirrors in crystal frames, and a passage carpeted in crimson, its panelled walls all white.'

Dimitry Markovich leapt from his chair.

'Why—you have been there, Anna Petrovna—'

Blushing and stammering, I told him about the accident with the barge.

'Your people were so kind, the housekeeper most of all. But I was a little girl. I asked no questions, and none of my father's people seemed to know much except the name of the manor. Your housekeeper did not say anything. I can't explain it—but I felt drawn towards her and wished I could meet her again.'

'I hope you will,' said Dimitry Markovich, bowed and went. My father said rather slowly:

'What a memory you have, little daughter! Lobchino! Agasha did not tell me much. I remember there were footmen. And someone telling me that maids were looking after you. Of course, Agasha remained. There are so many of these manors round about the neighbourhood. Fancy your remembering the housekeeper!'

'Nobody could forget her, Father.'

That is how it began. Dimitry Markovich left Moscow for his lands in Kaluga, and I found myself missing him. He returned. To my surprise and delight my father invited him to the Easter supper and fat Vlassovna triumphantly placed a huge dish of roast potatoes on the side table. Dimitry Markovich exchanged the triple Easter kiss with them all, and his 'foreign' clothes of pale lilac and grey did not bewilder them. When singing began, he joined in all the choruses. Dawn was breaking when I went to bed, tired but excited, and Agasha unbuttoned my silver *sarafán* and kissed my forehead.

After that? Well, there were walks, talks and curiously rewarding silences. Custom did not permit our driving out together, but custom did not stand in the way within the boundaries of Khlébnikovs. If my dear Agasha guessed at the truth, she kept her counsel, and Dimitry Markovich did not haunt our threshold. He never came uninvited, and on occasions he could not accept my father's offers of dinner or supper.

I was sixteen to his twenty-three, and what girl of sixteen could find reasons? For one thing, there were too many. Every hour spent in his company might have been compared with yet another opening petal of a big flower. He and I shared our love for Russia, the land and the people; we were interested in trees, plants, animals, birds and good literature, though he knew three foreign languages to my six. Dimitry Markovich confessed he had small use for poetry, and to my discomforture he knew mathematics, among which was a mystery called geometry that I had never heard of before.

It came out one June evening at supper, and my father laughed at my question:

'Pray, what is ge— ge—?'

'Dimitry Markovich, my daughter is at sea with common sums. Why, the other day she had to ask one of my clerks for help. There was a bill for some shoes made for her. One item was two roubles and other one rouble fifty copecks. Every time she tried to add them up, something different came out. I would not be surprised if one day she did not turn two and two into seven.'

He spoke so good-naturedly that I laughed, and Dimitry Markovich smiled.

'Well, sums are not easy for everyone. And I know no Latin at all. Anna Petrovna has talked to me of Virgil. He, I gather, was a great poet, and she has read him.' He bowed towards me and added, 'To me that would be far harder than geometry.'

By then I knew something of his background. I knew that he came of a wealthy family and had seven brothers and one sister. I had a vague idea that his father had been a singer. I knew no more.

Meanwhile, that honeyed summer went on. Agasha and another maid started preparing the best guest-chamber for my Aunt Mavra who was coming to us after the hay harvest in August.

On a hot July morning my skies darkened.

Dimitry Markovich came to make a hurried call. My father being busy, we two wandered off to the wilderness.

'I have to go to St. Petersburg,' sighed Dimitry Markovich. 'One of my brothers is getting married. So there will be dances and routs and so much time wasted!' He sighed again, and added: 'The Tsarina is coming to the wedding.'

I shot a bewildered glance at him.

'The Tsarina?'

'Why, yes. My two elder brothers are godsons of the late Empress Elizabeth. And there will be a great gathering of the clans. Please, be sorry for me. I so hate getting into satin and velvet and having my hair powdered. To hear my mother calling me *"mouzhik"* is not pleasant! I believe she imagines me living in a peasant hut!'

'A great gathering of the clans,' I repeated, my voice far from steady. 'Who are they?'

'Oh—my mother's people, the Dolgorukys,' he tossed at me

A.—8

indifferently. 'And so many others. My brother's bride is Princess Elizabeth Golitzina—'

'I wish them happy,' I mumbled.

'Oh I don't know. My brother is a soldier and she is supposed to be bad-tempered. Oh, Anna Petrovna, that wedding will be such a trial!'

'I am sure you will enjoy it.' I spoke woodenly.

I cannot remember what happened later. Dimitry Markovich went to say good-bye to my father and I fled to my room, a darkness in my mind. Wealth did not matter so much, but all those princes and counts raised a barrier. I remembered that earlier experience during a picnic on the Sparrow Hills.

'Fool that I am! I wish he had never come to Khlébnikovs! Merchants we are and merchants we stay! Dimitry Markovich is right to dislike poetry. It does make one's imagination run wild! As if such an idea would ever enter his head,' I said to myself, 'with all those grand relations of his!'

There was lead in my heart, but I kept my secret. Not even Agasha guessed at it. I was busy from sunrise till long after supper time. I sang, and helped Agasha to embroider the hand towels for my aunt, and danced in the kitchen at the sight of a pretty cake made by Vlassovna.

'Now don't you nibble it,' she said severely. 'It is for the feast,' but she was smiling and I kissed her and got a lump of pink sugar in return. Out in the yard I heard voices from the kitchen.

'Sunshine isn't in it!'

'She would make a cripple happy and no mistake!'

'And—'

'Now then,' Vlassovna's voice shouted, 'stop singing Anna's praises and get to work, wenches.'

One August morning before dinner I escaped to the wilderness to spend a little time bird-watching. I knew my feathered friends so well that often they would perch on my shoulders. But suddenly they flew away. I looked up and saw my father coming towards me, his face grave. He took my hand, led me to the little arbour, and I saw tears in his eyes.

'Dimitry Markovich is back in Moscow, little daughter. I have just left him in the book-room. He came to ask for your hand.' My father's voice was unsteady. 'I have given my consent, but it is for you to decide, child.'

I stared at a green and brown beetle in the grass; I heard the rustling of leaves overhead and a pigeon calling out to his mate. Then my eyes went misty and I clung to my father's arm.

'Well, Anna?'

'But how could I? He—he—he is a nobleman. His mother was born a princess. His brother has just married another—the Tsarina was there . . .'

'Yes! Dimitry Markovich had some private conversation with her and told her of his hopes. She said he would be a lucky man.'

'But—but,' I stammered, 'how could I marry into such a family? Never . . .'

'His father is as much of a born nobleman as I am. The late Empress Elizabeth ennobled him because of his wonderful voice. He grew up an ambitious man and married into the nobility, but he did not come from a merchant's stock, Anna. Mark Fedorovich's people were Ukrainian peasants. I believe his father bred horses and was a warm man, but he would not have known how to sign his name!'

'Still—'

'Look at me, child. Do you care for Dimitry Markovich?'

Mouth shaking, I raised my head. I knew that, contrary to the custom prevailing among us, my father would never compel me into marriage.

10

The Bells at St. Praskovia's

I once read in a German book that happy countries have no history, and did not believe it. I was certainly happy, but so many excitements fell to me daily and there was such a cheerful bustle at Khlébnikovs that I once said to Agasha:

'I wish there were forty-eight hours to a day! So much to think of and do.'

'You go to sleep, Anna. There is more wisdom in the morning than in the evening.'

There was Dimitry, then my dowry and the mysterious things my father's clerks called 'settlements'—presents to exult over and to thank people for. Finally, a few days after the Assumption feast, came our betrothal at St. Praskovia's. It was solemn, brief and very moving. On the *analóy* put in front of the altar gates, two plain gold rings lay on a cushion of green velvet. Only my father and one or two others were present. At a sign from the deacon Dimitry and I went up to the *analóy*. Father Vassily, in new green vestments given by my father, came through the side altar gate, made the sign of the cross over the rings and sprinkled them with blessed water. The deacon whispered to Dimitry to put his left hand on the cushion. Father Vassily slipped the ring on and said in a loud voice:

'Hereby is God's servant Dimitry betrothed to God's servant Anna.'

I heard the deacon whispering and stretched out my left hand. The same words were spoken, a prayer said, a blessing given, and we turned away. At our wedding those rings would be changed from the left hand to the right.

Dimitry and I left St. Praskovia's. We were affianced. A betrothal in the Orthodox church is far more binding than an engagement in the West. But we neither kissed nor held hands. That day Dimitry did not dine with us, and for the first time I was glad of it: I found two letters waiting for me at home. Both were sealed with the crest already known to me: a lyre surrounded by laurel leaves.

I took the letters into my room, looked at the unfamiliar handwriting and then at my left hand. It was such a comfort to see Dimitry's ring. 'We are betrothed! Nothing can change that!' I thought and broke one of the seals. The cold note, written in French, was proof enough to tell me what to expect from my in-laws. '*Mademoiselle*'—so my future mother-in-law chose to address me. In a few lines she explained that the state of her health would not permit her to attend her son's wedding, that she was sending me an icon of St. Dimitry set in pearls and hoped I would take great care of it. There was not a single word to wish me happiness. The signature was as formal as the beginning.

'If it were not a holy icon,' I thought, flinging the thick paper on the floor, 'I would throw it into the Yanza.'

I expected nothing better from my future father-in-law, and I proved right. He wrote a few lines in a barely legible hand. Unable to come to Moscow, he was sending me a small icon of St. Michael the Archangel. 'At Her Majesty's desire, we receive you into our family.'

'I don't want to meet any of them!' I cried angrily, went to find my father, and laid both letters before him. He shook his head.

'Sending you holy icons and writing such un-Christian letters! But I am glad to see that your eyes are dry.'

'Why should I cry? I am far too happy, Father.'

'Has Dimitry told you much about his parents?'

'Hardly anything.'

'That is as it should be. No son could say much about such parents. From all I hear, she is no great ornament to her rank and he is as proud as a peacock. God forgive them. But they are too busy quarrelling with each other to take much notice of their daughters-in-law. The Tsarina carried it off. Sit down, Anna, and don't waste yourself on anger. You will have to answer those absurd notes. One would do for two. I should write in French, begin "*Monsieur et Madame*," make no reference to their not coming to Moscow, thank them for the icons, and sign yourself "Anna Khlébnikova".' My father's shoulders shook with laughter. 'A surname which is every whit as good, if not better, as Poltoratzky. But say nothing to Dimitry.'

'I am glad he is not dining here today, Father. I should hate to have him see me angry.'

'But you must not be, little daughter. Now let us destroy those silly notes, shall we?'

It was left to a bride's parents to make arrangements for the wedding, but my father decided to consult me about everything, and Dimitry was present at all those discussions. He wondered which of the great Kremlin cathedrals I would choose, whether I would prefer the Metropolitan of Moscow or an archbishop to marry us, what guests to invite and what choir to engage.

I knew my father was looking at me. I did not laugh though I wanted to.

'I would like to be married by Father Vassily at St. Praskovia's. The nuns sing well enough. My Aunt Mavra will be staying here, and she can be matron of honour. You choose your two best men, Dimitry. I want no other guests except our household here and you can bring the people you have to Lobchino, particularly Mavra Akimovna. I would like us to be married in the evening— such is the custom among merchant folk, Dimitry. We will have the wedding supper here—together with all your people and my father's. Do you approve?'

Dimitry bowed.

'And then we will travel to my place near Kaluga. Is that what you would wish, Anna?'

'Oh yes!'

My father nodded.

'St. Praskovia's let it be. I will arrange things with Father Vassily. And what about the date?'

A calendar was spread on the table. I looked at it gloomily. Vigils and fasts and vigils again when no weddings might be held. Then the autumn slush, *sliákost*, the deep mud on the roads reaching up to the axles, and the journey from Moscow to Kaluga would be impossible. Dimitry looked so ill at ease that it was my duty as well as my pleasure to keep cheerful.

'Let it be the first week of Christmas then! Good sledge weather and, my dear, I am going to be so busy—time will just fly.' I prattled on: 'My aunt will be here very soon and I know she will expect me to embroider every piece of bed-linen and spend ages examining the presents. Oh—and tell stories, too! You will like her, Dimitry, and you don't mind my choosing St. Praskovia's, do you?'

'Mind? I would wed you in a cellar,' he said.

Dimitry followed me to the kitchen-garden and I led the way to the little arbour.

'My very dear,' I began, 'your wife-to-be has a favour to ask of you. Take me to Lobchino. I know Mavra Akimovna and others will be at our wedding, but I would so like to see her before. I don't suppose she remembers me—'

'Indeed she does,' Dimitry broke in. 'She has told me how very courteous you were, but could you ever be anything else?'

'Rubbish! I can be cross, unmannerly and angry!'

'Have it your way, dear heart. My dear Mavrusha is so happy about our betrothal. She is busily stitching at a present for you. Yes, of course, we will drive over. I am staying there now and it is all comfortable. My cook had been trained by a Frenchman.'

I shook my head.

'I'd so much rather have the common Russian food, Dimitry, *pelméni* or something like that.'

'I will tell him. Dear heart, Lobchino will be your *pied-à-terre* whenever we come to Moscow—'

'Yes, yes,' I broke in, 'but, Dimitry, when we drive over there before our wedding would you very much mind having Mavra Akimovna at table with us?'

He burst out laughing.

'Mind? Dear heart, my Mavrusha sups with me whenever I am there. Anna, would you like her to join us at Avchourino?'

I hesitated.

'Agasha would come with us. They met and liked each other, I think. But, Dimitry, I'd so much rather Agasha stayed on at Khlébnikovs to look after my father.'

'Things will get arranged. I won't have you fret, dear heart.'

Soon my Aunt Mavra reached Khlébnikovs. I heard her voice in the porch as she thanked all the saints that nothing untoward had happened to her on the perilous journey from Nijny-Novgorod. I heard Agasha's reply as she piloted her to the guest-chamber, but my aunt chose to make straight for my room. Plump and rosy, wrapped in a blue travelling cloak, she walked in, kissed me warmly and settled herself on my bed.

'The wenches are bringing my trunks in. There will be a trifle or two for you, niece,' she panted. 'Now the deacon read my brother's letter to me. Is he a prince or a count?'

'Who?' I asked foolishly.

'Well, then, you are in love and no mistake! Fancy not knowing!'

'He has no title, Aunt Mavra.'

'Just as well.' She nodded her shawled head. 'Believe it or not, a neighbour's daughter fell for someone, a real dandy he looked, prattling about balls and what not in the capital, and he wore brocade waistcoats and had his head powdered, I ask you! Well, the wench was a fool. Not so her father! He soon found out that the dandy had been a flunkey in some grand house or other. Well, I think the girl wept a bit, but no harm was done,' she laughed. 'Getting married at Christmas, are you? Not much time left, is there? At St. Praskovia's? That is good. I do like Father Vassily. But there is your dowry, niece—bed linen, table linen and what not besides. And I must see Vlassovna. A wedding supper is not a cobweb to be blown off—with the guests and all. Not a pedlar's marriage, niece, yours is going to be.'

'Aunt Mavra,' I broke in—but she swept on.

'I did think you might be married in some cathedral, and I have had my purple velvet gown packed and all. Why, your father wrote that the young man's brother had been wedded to someone so grand—a Metropolitan marrying them and the Tsarina coming! Now that I think of it St. Praskovia's is a nice enough church for a Sunday Mass—but not for a grand wedding! How could I wear my purple velvet there? What will the guests say?'

I told her who were coming. Her eyes bulged.

'And what does the groom say?' she gasped. 'Looks to me like planting a turnip upside down.'

'He said he would marry me in a cellar,' I laughed.

'Is he not right in his head then?'

'The cleverest man ever,' I assured her. My aunt shook her head so violently that the shawl slipped off.

'And where is he taking you after the wedding?'

'Why, here. There will be a grand supper for all our people and a few of his. Then he and I are going to his estate near Kaluga. Aunt Mavra, he has a wonderful coach—called a *dormeuse*. You can eat and sleep there. He has very good horses and he is taking twelve outriders all armed, so nothing untoward is likely to happen.'

My aunt pulled the glove off her right hand and crossed herself three times.

'You will look splendid in your purple velvet and pearls.'

She sighed.

'With your Ivan and his ilk to look at them.'

'Aunt Mavra! There will be Father and Dimitry—'

She looked at me rather curiously.

'Not one of his own folk coming! Anna, did he get his father's consent?'

'Surely—you had it all in the letter. The Tsarina suggested it.'

'And he is rich—not that you need wealth.'

'He has a manor near Moscow and a huge estate in the province of Kaluga.'

'A warm man,' admitted my aunt and hoisted herself off my bed. 'Now come to my room, Anna, and have a look at the trifles I have brought for you.'

The 'trifles' made me gasp. In a big box inlaid with amber and lined with crimson velvet lay a pearl necklace, a pair of ruby ear-rings, an emerald pin, four gold bracelets studded with sapphires, a turquoise buckle, and a rose-satin purse filled with gold coins.

'Aunt Mavra, you should not.'

'When you have done admiring the knicknacks, you might remember that your aunt is famished,' she said severely. 'Nothing but a couple of *báranki* and a pickled cucumber have I had today.'

I flew to the door. In less than ten minutes my aunt sat down at the table in the *górnitza*, praised all she saw, and demolished most of it with a remarkable rapidity. When Agasha came in with a bowl of stewed apples, my aunt beamed, and kissed her warmly.

'But your women won't take it amiss if I go to the kitchens and the linen-room? There is my niece's dowry, Agasha, and the wedding supper too. Not the matters for a man to think of!' She laughed, her white teeth gleaming. 'Why, your master would not know if you gave him a stewed leather belt for dinner! All men are alike!' She sighed, plunged her spoon into the apples, and said gravely: 'Now, Agasha, we are like so many pickled herrings at Khlébnikovs! St. Praskovia's, I ask you!'

Agasha did not smile.

'It was Anna's choice, Mavra Mikhaylovna—'

'I know,' sighed my aunt. 'Sit you down, Agasha. Now my late husband had a niece and she married one Zhukov, a soap merchant in Kazan. Well, they had one daughter, and whom did *she* marry? Some Tatar or other! And her with a dowry as good as Anna's. We did not know what to make of it! A few months back I heard about the girl. That Tatar had died, and she was minding geese on someone's farm. And she—my husband's niece—' Aunt Mavra finished the apples and beamed. 'Seeing your father is away from home, I think I had better go to bed. A long journey does not make for clear wit, my dear, and you might just as well expect a mountain to come to you as a wedding to prepare itself on its own!'

It was a warm August evening, and the tall trees girdling the wilderness were burnished gold. In the kitchen-garden, plums and apples were already turning roseate. Here and there candles glimmered in our men's lodgings over the long row of store-houses. Semka's daughter, her scarlet kirtle blown about her bare legs, ran towards the well-head, her right arm swinging a bucket. The big dogs lay on the cobbles, lazily swishing their tails. Someone had forgotten to latch a store-room door; it creaked plaintively, until I heard a voice.

'Fekla, ah Fekla, see to that latch.'

The kitchen windows stood wide open—Vlassovna was scolding a girl.

'Scrub the mess, will you? And how do I fry eggs tomorrow—'

'There are hundreds more in the larder,' replied a shrill young voice.

'Good at counting, are you? Get your bucket and besom.'

Those were commonplace bits and pieces of the life led at Khlébnikovs, but that evening they seemed very precious. I leant out of my casement. I heard my aunt's measured snoring, I heard Agasha and others make for their supper in the kitchen. The evening was closing in. I lit a candle and slipped into the book-room. There were many treasures of my own on my father's shelves. I meant to do some sorting out. I did none. I slumped down by the little table close to a window-sill, snuffed out the candle, and sat still. My father was supping with some friends in the German Quarter. My aunt was asleep and I knew that the folk in the kitchen would not hurry over their supper.

Panic seized me. How could I, a girl of sixteen, manage a large household? I did my small share at Khlébnikovs, but I found help on the right hand and on the left. Agasha and Vlassovna between them ran the place. I could stitch, hem and darn—always under Agasha's supervision. I had never ordered a meal in my life. Vlassovna welcomed me in her kingdom, taught me to make butter, to prepare fruit for jam and for bottling, to get the ingredients together for the stuffing of poultry, but I knew I was far more clumsy than the girl Vlássovna had scolded for smashing a few eggs. There was a milk cheese my father liked. I knew nothing about it except that it was pleasant to eat.

There would be far more than that. I tried to imagine the house. Avchourino, Dimitry had said, had been built by Rastrelli. His father had never lived there, preferring his estates to be nearer St. Petersburg. Dimitry had not said very much about it except that the grounds were magnificent. What could a chit of sixteen do in a mansion? I shuddered at the idea of losing myself in that immensity.

And there was my father. How could I leave him? Agasha, if she stayed, would see to his comfort, but she was not his daughter. Vlassovna and the others were loyal and hardworking. But was it enough? He had many friends, but his work as a merchant and his studies made large demands on his time. I hated the idea of his sitting alone in the *górnitza* or in the book-room, with two hireling clerks next door, bent over their ledgers, copying out endless invoices for corn and seeds. I wept.

So he found me, a big wax candle in a bronze stick in his hand. 'Little daughter, here in the dark? You should be in bed.'

'I can't marry Dimitry. I could not leave you, Father.'

He put the candlestick on the table, sat down by me, and threw an arm in its wide sleeve across my shoulders. I poured it all out.

'Your dear mother,' he said very gently, 'was sixteen when she married me. Her people, as you know, were far more wealthy than ours. She was the only child and had three bachelor uncles who were good men, but they lived on their lands and rather aped the gentry. It all came to her and some day will be yours. We were wedded at Archangel cathedral in the Kremlin. Her father was nicknamed "the linen Czar". But she took to the humbler ways of Khlébnikovs like a duck to water. Except for your dowry, your case is just the reverse. I know you will manage. Your

bridegroom and I had a long talk about it. He is determined that
you should not neglect your studies. There are good people at
that place, hard-working and loyal. They will welcome a mistress
if but for her manners. I have seldom praised you, little daughter,
but it always pleased me to hear your thanks for the least service
done for you.'

'But to leave you all alone, Father,' I gulped.

'Listen, Anna. I asked your aunt not to tell you just yet. She
has come here for good. Khlébnikovs used to be her home in her
youth. It will be so again. Everything is arranged. I believe she
will be happy to end her days in Moscow. And, after all, little
daughter, Kaluga is not at the end of the world. I trust that great
mansion will have a room or two to spare for your old father and
his sister. Now, off to bed with you!'

Comforted, I pressed my lips to his hand and slipped out of the
room.

Dimitry came to dine the next day. My Aunt Mavra in a yellow
kófta and a wide brown kirtle looked at him and burst out:

'Well, nephew-to-be, I must say you don't look like one of the
St. Petersburg fops. Thank God for that! I hear they paint their
faces.'

'I prefer to wash mine,' said Dimitry gravely.

She got up and embraced him. He answered her kiss, and,
stooping, kissed her hand.

'Anna's mother would have been glad of you, God rest her
dear soul.'

I knew they were friends.

At dinner Aunt Mavra said to my father:

'I have been everywhere, brother. In the kitchen and larders
and store-rooms. Sterling people you have got to serve you.'

'I know they are sterling, sister.'

'Vlassovna says you don't like pepper! No wonder! I well
remember how you emptied the pepper-pot into Aunt Liza's tea,
and she coughed and sneezed for hours. You did get a flogging,
brother.'

'What a memory you have! Now, what about a little more pike,
sister?'

'Thank you, and some egg sauce, please.' Aunt Mavra beamed
at Dimitry and me. 'Now, dears, I am fond of my victuals, that

I am. Take care of your stomach and all shall go well. There was a wealthy enough widow at Nijny and a wench of mine was cousin to her cook. Poor woman!' sighed my aunt. 'Rolling in money and all, and she lived on thin gruel and cabbage soup. She died before was fifty, and no wonder.'

'There is a stuffed goose coming, sister,' said my father gravely.

Aunt Mavra enjoyed her victuals and she liked gossip but oh she could work, and a family wedding gave her plenty of scope. In the following weeks she got my dowry ready and neatly packed in numberless valises.

'Oh, niece! Twelve armed postilions! Enough to send a band of brigands packing! You will be as safe as a hare in her form. Vlassovna is a jewel! I went to see her this morning and I said, "A wedding supper is no joke, Vlassovna", and she said, "Don't you worry, Mavra Mikhaylovna. Nothing will be forgotten. Agasha and Fekla will clean the silver service. It will be fit for the Tsarina,"' and here my aunt stopped and sighed. 'I do wish the Tsarina were coming, Anna.'

'I don't think Dimitry would like the fuss,' I told her. I felt grateful for everything.

One golden September morning a chaise carried us to Lobchino —Aunt Mavra, Dimitry, Agasha and me. My dear Dimitry did not know that I had a lengthy argument with my aunt.

'Go to that manor! Certainly not! I have heard of it! There will be flunkeys and velvet carpets and what not!'

'Agasha is coming.'

'That is as it should be.'

'And there is a very dear friend of Dimitry's to welcome us.'

Aunt Mavra pursed her lips.

'Don't look like that. His housekeeper. I hope some day she may come to Avchourino.'

'There will be foreign food! I am not used to it. My stomach—'

'Aunt Mavra, you will see foreign furnishings and clothes, but the meal will be Russian, Dimitry has promised.'

'I have never been inside a manor! Not a place for a merchant's widow to poke her nose in.'

In the end, however, Aunt Mavra put on her best fawn cloth kirtle, a brown satin *kófta*, adorned herself with several turquoise ornaments and challenged me:

'Well, do I look fit for that precious manor?'

'You could not look better.'

Lobchino was farther than I had thought. In fact, except for that sapphire velvet room, I could not remember it at all. Aunt Mavra sat up very erect and, usually garrulous, she said nothing beyond remarking that the weather was fine. Agasha sat facing me, her face wreathed in smiles. She wore a dark blue *sarafán* and a grey kirtle, a red-spotted kerchief on her head.

I smiled back, but I felt far from easy. Aunt Mavra and the mid-day meal at Lobchino. . . . I did not know that Dimitry had made all the arrangements least likely to upset my father's sister.

The coachman reined in. There were no velvet-coated flunkeys near the porch. There stood a slim, tall woman, whose face I still remembered, but her clothes were not 'foreign'. She wore a dark red *sarafán* and a blue kirtle, with pale blue kerchief on her head. Dimitry jumped out of the chaise. She bowed from the hips and bent to kiss his hand but he caught hold of her shoulders, kissed her on both cheeks, and cried out:

'I have brought your mistress to be, Mavrusha dear, and her aunt and her nannie! Please do all the honours. I must see to the horses.'

He turned and helped us out of the chaise. Mavra Akimovna bowed again and wanted to kiss my hand, but I forestalled her by kissing her on both cheeks. As to my aunt, she at once called her 'Mavrusha', asked for her surname, and plunged into reminiscences about a most capable shoemaker in Kolomna.

'He would be my uncle, Mavra Mikhaylovna.'

No flunkeys in velvet coats were to be seen. Two men in white blouses and wide dark blue knee-breeches, known as *sharováry*, served a wholly national meal starting with *bortch* and ending with apple *oládiy*. Later, we went over the manor, but by then my aunt was reconciled to the 'foreign' furniture, velvet carpets and all. Lobchino had no park. The garden was a tidy riot of flowers, fruit trees and vegetables. Beyond stretched the fields, some of which Dimitry meant to plant with *kartóshka*.

All in all, it was a blissfully unwrinkled day, and my own pleasure was heightened on hearing that Mavrusha was to join Dimitry and me at Avchourino. I felt that such a kind and capable woman would soon become a friend.

Back at Khlébnikovs, when the chaise had carried Dimitry back to Lobchino, Aunt Mavra admitted she had never had such a pleasant outing.

'In spite of the flunkeys,' my father teased her.

'I never saw one, brother. There was just one thing: those foreign chairs—their legs were so slender I quite expected they would give way under me! But everything else was so pleasant that I kept forgetting them.'

I was glad that my aunt would stay on at Khlébnikovs. I gave a coffee party for my friends at the German Quarter, and thanked them all, particularly Mitzi, for their presents. Poor Mitzi's gift was a horror: a square piece of bright yellow cloth embroidered with impossible pink pansies. 'My own work,' murmured Mitzi modestly and I kissed her. I think the bright yellow horror ended by being greatly cherished by Fekla.

Only wisps of memories remain of that time. I walked in a maze. I no longer worried about the responsibilities of becoming mistress in a grand mansion. In fact I had no worries. Dimitry came every day. Sometimes we talked and laughed. Oftener we stayed silent, satisfied with being together. My father and aunt, to say nothing of the household, may well have thought me odd during that time. Once at supper, I poured vinegar over the stewed apples. Aunt Mavra stared.

'You are not feeling ill, Anna, or anything?'

My father laughed.

'Certainly not, sister. Her mind is full of Dimitry but, little daughter, he is not like a bottle of vinegar.'

Days and weeks ran on and on, and Christmas was upon us. Two days later, white-gowned and veiled, I knelt before my father in the *górnitza*. He blessed me with an icon. Then someone threw a sable cloak over my shoulders, and I think two of our men carried me to the sledge waiting outside the gates. At St. Praskovia's I caught a glimpse of my aunt, resplendent in her purple velvet and pearls. There was Dimitry waiting, in pearl grey coat and breeches and a pink brocade waistcoat, his hair unpowdered, his face grave.

'It is my very own wedding,' I thought and wondered if it were a dream.

I heard the deacon's deep voice, the nuns' responses, I saw

Father Vassily's kind, thin face as he stood exchanging our rings.

Then we drove back, but I can remember little of the supper, the cheers, the clapping and singing. I came out of the dream when my booted feet touched the crisp snow, and I saw the *dormeuse*, turned, saw my father, fell on his neck, and heard his gentle voice:

'All shall go well, little daughter. God bless you.'

Then I stepped into the *dormeuse* and found it warm and comfortable. Dimitry, now my husband, followed me and the horses started.

'I hope you will like your home, dear heart. It faces the Oka. Rastrelli built the house. He is supposed to be a genius.'

'But you have not married a genius,' I murmured and felt too happy to say any more.

Epilogue

Anna Poltoratzky had thirty-two years of happiness with her husband. She took to the splendours of Avchourino in the province of Kaluga like a duck to water. She picked up the intricate threads of a huge household as easily as she picked up languages. Her parents-in-law never met her and both died soon after her marriage, but Anna made great friends with their seven sons and one daughter, Elizabeth.

Piotr Khlébnikov died in 1792, having bequeathed some of his books and manuscripts to the Empress Catherine. Anna journeyed to Moscow and brought back her Aunt Mavra to end her days at Avchourino. Anna disposed of Khlébnikovs, taking great care that all her father's folk were provided for. But she did not like travelling. She seldom went to Moscow. She did not visit St. Petersburg till 1816 to make arrangements for her son, Serge, my grandfather, to stay with his Aunt Elizabeth, married to Alexis Olenin, the first director of the Imperial library.

Anna's energy was incredible. To the six languages she had learned before her marriage, she added two more—Turkish and Arabic. She had six daughters and one son. Her father's death left her sole owner of seven large and scattered estates. She had English governesses for her daughters and enjoyed the help of Mr. Jennings as her manager in chief. As she got older, she seemed to miss Yasha, her brother. After some years in England he had gone to live in America, where he opened a small school for boys as well as a bookshop. He never returned to Russia. His letters were brief and infrequent. Under Catherine's successor, the Emperor Paul I, foreign correspondence was banned. Anna had a habit of making marginal remarks in some of her books. One such came to her descendants and carried a wistful note: 'I wish I knew if Yasha had any children.'

Dimitry and she entertained lavishly but wisely. Neighbours' visits were a duty. Friends brought pleasure. Great scholars came

to Avchourino to use the Khlébnikov library so enlarged by the uncles' collections that eight great rooms were needed to house it all. Among such guests was the famous historian, Karamzin.

Unlike all his brothers, Dimitry had never been in the Guards. He was well over fifty at the beginning of the Napoleonic wars. He and Anna together sent a donation of ten million silver roubles for the war expenses and equipped a big battalion of their own peasants. The unit came to be called the Poltoratzky battalion and the tablet with the names of the fallen used to hang on the wall of a Moscow church. During the Napoleonic invasion of Russia, Dimitry and Anna stayed at Avchourino. The unexpected retreat of La Grande Armée in October 1812 ravaged the province of Kaluga, and one French unit wandered off the main road and looted Avchourino. Her governesses, in their old age, used to say that Anna kept a heroic calm all through that difficult time.

Dimitry died in 1818 and his only son Serge, aged fifteen, became the owner of one of the largest fortunes in Russia. Anna was a devoted mother to all her children, but Serge was the apple of her eye. Early enough she foresaw a scholar in him. Much against her own will she sent him to St. Petersburg where he was page to the Empress Elizabeth, wife of Alexander I. Later, his soldier uncles insisted on his entering the Preobrazhensky Guards, but to Anna's relief her son's military career was short. He gave up his commission as a second lieutenant (*práporchik*), devoted himself to literature and made friends with Pushkin, Zhukovsky and others.

Anna saw three of her daughters married to men she approved of. Two others died unwed in the late twenties of the nineteenth century.

Anna stayed on at Avchourino, playing hostess to her son's visitors, reading, gardening, looking after animals and birds, receiving reports from Mr. Jennings and the bailiffs. Her energies seemed inexhaustible: through all the four seasons she got up at five a.m., washed in cold water, dressed herself, and came down to her coffee and rolls. Wet or fine, she went out for a stroll before getting back to the work of letters and interviews with Mr. Jennings and his assistants. Anna looked after the peasants and their livestock. Wild animals and birds meant much to her. She knew that wolves must be killed but she would not allow a bear to be touched.

In the late 1830s Anna began feeling oddly tired. She had never been ill in her life and had never consulted a doctor. Now she asked for advice and took to wearing spectacles. Miss Saunders, once her daughters' governess and now her friend, begged her to stay in bed a little longer. 'I must go on running the household,' Anna told her.

She ran it most efficiently until 1843. One early April morning she had a basket filled with bread-crumbs to feed her birds and went out into the lower meadow to admire the spring flowers. She came back and stumbled on the steps of the porch. Two footmen caught her up. 'Into the little rose-room,' Anna said to them. 'There is a comfortable sofa and, please, send Agasha to me.'

Agasha had been gone for many years. The men fetched Miss Mason and Miss Saunders. Anna smiled at them.

'I am all right, but I could not mount the stairs. Please, have a table and an armchair placed by that window.'

Anna never left the rose-room again. A comfortable bed was arranged for her and she spent many hours at the table by the window, scribbling, reading, or bird-gazing. She had so many feathered friends in the grounds. One day in early May Miss Saunders found her, the quill fallen out of her hand, her lace-capped head leant against the chair back, deep peace on her face. A sheet of paper on the table carried an unfinished sentence: 'How good to know Dimitry, our daughters and I will soon be together. God bless S . . .' the single letter undoubtedly meaning her son Serge. He and her daughter Vera, married to Alexander Liarsky, were the only ones left at the time, but Vera was ill at her home in the Smolensk province and Serge was abroad.

The Khlébnikovs were extinct, and not a single Poltoratzky attended Anna's funeral. In a way it would have pleased her. There had been no fuss at her wedding, there was none at the funeral—nothing but the deep grief of the household and the peasants for a good, generous and fair-dealing mistress.

A week later Miss Mason, taking fresh flowers to the grave, saw a small brown bear walking away. He must have been one of Anna's many four-footed friends.

The material for this book has been gathered from many sources. There was the *Le Bulletin Bibliographique Poltoratzky*, written and published privately by my late aunt, Contessa Filippani-Ronconi, *née* Poltoratzky, in Rome in 1910. Information about Piotr Khlébnikov and Khlébnikovs came from the copious notes made by another aunt, Fanny Poltoratzky, who obviously meant to write a book about her grandmother, but who died in 1916, the work never completed. Khlébnikovs and, indeed, most of Kolomna, where the houses were all timbered, perished in the great fire of Moscow in 1812. Avchourino, long since gone out of the family, was burned down during the peasant riots of 1905.

There was a mass of oral tradition, handed down from generation to generation. The letters patent of untitled nobility, signed by Catherine the Great, and issued to my great-great-grandfather, Piotr Mikhaylovich Khlébnikov, *'Kolómensky Koopetz'*, i.e. 'a merchant of Kolomna', were in my mother's possession. 'We, Catherine, by the grace of God etc, etc, hereby confer the honour

... for his singular and valuable services to the literary enlightenment of the Empire . . .' My mother also possessed a very modest
signet of her great-grandfather—a sheaf of corn, surrounded by
tiny laurel leaves, engraved on agate and mounted on a thin gold
ring. All these items perished in Russia.

But at least one of Anna's personal possessions is in safe-
keeping in England. It is one of her many blotters made of stout
homespun linen. I gave it to my friend, Mr. J. S. G. Simmons of
All Souls College, Oxford, whose unflagging interest in the
Poltoratzky matters has greatly encouraged me to write the
family chronicles.

For this reason *Anna* is dedicated to him.

E. M. Almedingen.

Somerset, March 1971

Glossary

Akimovna   (Adj., f.) Patronymic, literally, 'daughter of Akim'. Among peasantry, married women and widows were more often than not addressed in such a way.

Análoy   (N., masc., sing.) A square, slightly sloping table with a ledge at one end and very high legs. It would be placed in front of the altar gates and used for service books etc. Covered with a silk or velvet cloth.

Bába   (N., f., sing.) A tall, round cake baked at Easter. Of light texture. Many eggs were used for the mixture. When baked, it would be covered with a thin layer of white or pink icing-sugar.

Baránki   (N., f., plural) Kind of wheaten rusk made in the shape of a bracelet.

Báryshna   (N., f., sing.) Miss, daughter of a gentleman.

Bortch   (N. masc., sing. Never used in plural.) Soup made of beetroot boiled, carefully mashed and blended with thin cream. In Ukraina, *bortch* used to be served with pieces of sausage or bacon.

Boússý   (N., f., plural. Singular, *boussinka*, hardly ever used.) Beads made of silver, brass, copper, porcelain, or coloured glass. Such necklaces used to be in great demand at every fair in the past.

Clergy marriages   In the Orthodox church at the time, men had to be married before ordination. Once widowed, they could not remarry. Priesthood and diaconate were separate. A deacon never became a priest but he might, if he had a good voice, reach the rank of an archdeacon. His duties were to chant litanies, read the Hours, and assist the priest, but he did not administer the sacraments. A secular priest might be raised to the rank of an archpriest but he could never become a bishop. Bishops were elected from among monks and were celibates.

Donskoy Abbey   A large monastery on the way to Kolomensky Palace, dedicated to St. Dimitry Donskoy, Prince of Moscow, who was the first to defeat the Tatars on the field of Kulikovo in 1380. The victory did not end the Tatar Yoke, begun in 1240, but it greatly weakened it.

Dormeuse   (From the French.) A coach designed for sleeping in.

Górnitza   (N., f., sing.) In general terms, any room in the house. In this case, a room set apart for meals and entertaining.

Grísha   (N., masc.) Diminutive of *Grigoriy*, i.e. Gregory. Among peasantry, the diminutive usually ended in *ka*, i.e. *Grishka, Petka*—i.e. diminutive of *Piotr,* Peter; *Mashka* for *Masha*, diminutive of Maria, etc.

Kalách   (N., masc., sing. Plural *kaláchi*.) A wheaten loaf specially favoured in Moscow. Very light, shaped like an oval purse with a handle. Floured on top. Usually baked at home and eaten hot, lavishly buttered.

Kamzól   (N., masc., sing. Origin doubtful, probably German.) A coat reaching no further than the waist.

Karaváy   (N., masc., sing.) A flattish round loaf of rye bread.

Kartóshka   From German *kartoffeln*. The name given to potatoes, introduced in Russia by my great-grandfather, Dimitry Poltoratzky. By the end of the eighteenth century, *kartóshka* became a staple of the peasant diet.

Khlébnik	From *khlieb,* i.e. bread. Baker.
Khramóvniki	One of the Moscow districts.
Khristós Voskrésse	(i.e. 'Christ is risen'.) The traditional Easter greeting.
Kibítka	A hooded carriage usually drawn by three horses, *troyka.*
Klobúk	A tall black headgear worn by clergy. (The bishop's was white.) The nuns' *klobuk* was covered by a thin black veil reaching down to the shoulders.
Kófta	(N., fem., sing. Origin unknown.) A blouse with long sleeves reaching below the waist.
Kolómensky, Koopetz	(Adj. and n., masc., sing.) A merchant of Kolomna.
Kolymáza	A huge unwieldy coach drawn by four and sometimes six horses.
Kooptchíka	A merchant's wife.
Kooptchík	A merchant's son, a young merchant.
Kulich	A round, tallish cake, baked at Easter, heavier than a *bába*; richly stuffed with raisins, sultanas, candied peel, chopped almonds and nutmeg. It used to be the fashion to put it on the table, a paper pink rose stuck in the middle. The quality of a *kulich* often determined the economic status of a household. 'They had no almonds in their *kulich*! Just fancy!' Almonds were imported and cost dear in Russia.
Kvas	The favourite national drink of the past, slightly

intoxicating, made either of rye bread or of berries. Raspberry *kvas* was particularly liked in Ukraina.

Mouzhik (N., masc., sing.) A peasant. Any 'unpolished' person, i.e. someone walking into a drawing-room, his boots muddy, etc.

Moy ray (*Ray*—n., masc., sing. *ra*, pronounced as a long 'a'.) My paradise.

Nemétzkaya Slobodá The foreigners' quarter on the banks of the Yanza.

Novodievechy Convent. One of the abbeys within the Kremlin gates.

Oládiy (N., fem., plural.) Sliced apples fried in butter, a favourite pudding.

Páskha (N., fem., sing.) A pyramidal confection made of sweetened *tvorog* (solidified milk), passed through a sieve, flavoured with vanilla, chopped almonds and candied peel.

Pável Paul.

Pavlínovoye From *paylin,* a peacock—ad., neut. In the present case, Peacocks' Court.

Pelméni (N., always used in plural.) Small, oval shaped pieces of well-rolled pastry with a tiny bit of minced meat or chicken inside, folded over, boiled in slightly salted water and well strained.

Pétka (*see* Grisha)

Pétrovna (*see* Akimovna)

Piotr Peter.

Piróg (N. masc., sing. Plural *pirógi.*) A large square or oblong pastry filled with meat, or fish, or eggs, or any vegetables. A sweet *piróg* had either jam or stewed apples. A small *piróg* was called *pirozhók*, n., masc., sing.-plural *pirozkhi*, and was usually served with soup.

Podmoskóvnaya (Adj. fem., sing.) Literally, 'under (*pod*) Moscow'. An estate lying in the environs of Moscow.

Pogrebétz (N., masc., sing. Plural *pogrebtzy*.) A case made either of leather, wood, or sometimes silver, used for provisions during a journey since a great many inns offered nothing except liquor or hot water (*kipiatok*) for tea.

Polúshubok (N., masc., sing.) A man's short winter coat, barely reaching the knees, made of thick cloth, lined with fur and having a broad fur collar.

Potómstvenniy dvorianiñ (Adj. and n., masc. sing.) Literally, a 'hereditary gentleman'.

Práportchik (N., masc., sing.) Second lieutenant in foot guards or infantry regiments.

Prístav (N., masc., sing.) A senior policeman.

Pustósh (N., fem., sing. Very seldom used in plural.) Land gone to waste; never used as pasture or arable; usually covered with shrub and scutch; a wilderness. Some such places were due to total lack of drainage. Others were allowed to turn into *pustósh* if a murder had been committed there and popular imagination peopled the place with ghouls, ghosts and devils. But at Khlébnikovs, the *putosh,* according to Anna, was something of a rough pleasance and trees grew at its end.

Razgovlénie (N., neut., sing.) Easter night supper, the food having been blessed by the priest after the service.

Russkáya (Adj., fem. Always in singular.) A national dance.

Samovár (N., masc., sing.) A tea-urn, literally, 'self-boiler'. It had a funnel in the middle where kindling would be put. Between the funnel and the outer walls there was enough space for cold water to be poured in. A tap was fixed towards the end of the urn. Once kindling was lit, the *samovár* had a bent iron funnel put on top and placed under the open chimney. Tea would be made from boiling water and then the tea-pot would be placed on top 'to stand'. A *samovár* would be made of brass, copper, or silver. A well-to-do peasant considered himself wealthy if he possessed one of copper. The best *samovár* makers were at Tula.

Sarafán (N., masc.). The traditional woman's garment falling just above the knees, its sleeves reaching down to the elbow. A *sarafán* was open in front to show a linen blouse. It could be made of cotton or of brocade. In wealthy merchant houses, it would have jewelled buttons and gold embroidery. It continued forming a part of court dress until 1917.

Sený (N., plural.) Never used in singular. A stoutly timbered porch of a merchant's or a peasant's house. Sometimes it had an outer door, sometimes not. Usually made of oak.

Sharováry (Always used in the plural.) Very wide trousers, always worn tucked into knee-high boots.

Shúba (N., fem.) A winter coat worn by men and women, reaching down to the ankles, with a deep fur collar, made of thick cloth and lined with fur throughout. Fox was cheap; bearskin was dearer, but sable was the choicest of all. A sable-lined *shúba* was an important item of a bride's dowry.

Sliákost (N., fem.) Autumn mud which made travelling impossible.

Tsarskiya Vrata (Adj. and n. Always used in plural.) Literally,

'Tsar's gates'. An altar in the Orthodox Church is a room (the Western altar is called 'The Sacrifice Table'), separated from the rest of the church by a wall with three doors, 'Tsar's gates' being in the middle. Only priests can go through them.

Tsárskoe Seló A village with two places, a great park, and several churches, to the west of St. Petersburg. The favourite resort of Catherine the Great. In her day, the whole of the park was open to the public.

Válenky (N., plural.) Knee-high thick felt boots worn in winter by men, women, and children.

Vatrúshka (N., fem., sing.) A small, round, open tart filled with *tvorog*, jam, or stewed apples.

Velikán (N., masc., sing.) A giant.

Velikiy Post (Adj. or n., masc.) Literally, the Great Fast, i.e. Lent. In Russia it began on a Monday, called the Pure Monday, and not on a Wednesday. It used to be kept most rigorously. For seven weeks no meat, poultry, eggs, cheese, butter, milk appeared at a table. Honey served for sugar. Fish, if fried, had to be done in vegetable oil. Sugar was banned since animal bones were used for its refining. Meals were limited to two a day— midday dinner and a meagre supper. There were no weddings, balls, or theatres.

Verstá A land measure, a little less than a mile.

Vlassovna i.e. a daughter of Vlass.

Yasha Diminutive of *Yákov*, i.e. Jacob.

Yatagan Short curved sword.

Zaútrenia Easter night service.

Zhban (Obsolete, n., masc.) A goblet of glass, silver, or gold.